The Songster of Javensbee

S. J. Riccobono

Order this book online at www.trafford.com
or email orders@trafford.com

Most Trafford titles are also available at major online book retailers.

Printed in Victoria, BC, Canada.

ISBN: 978-1-4269-2117-9 (sc)

*Our mission is to efficiently provide the world's finest, most comprehensive book publishing
service, enabling every author to experience success. To find out how to publish your
book, your way, and have it available worldwide, visit us online at www.trafford.com*

Trafford rev. 02/04/2010

 www.trafford.com

North America & international
toll-free: 1 888 232 4444 (USA & Canada)
phone: 250 383 6864 ♦ fax: 812 355 4082

ONE

FONDLY DESIRED BY THE YOUNG, their families and lovers alike, the wooded planet offered a safe resort to those seeking adventure. Night time shuttles passed over sparkling fire pits where children huddled near flames instantly tempered by the cooler air around them. One such pit drew a mother with a tray full of hot drinks served up to grabbing hands. Tray empty, she retreated back to the modular shelters near the edge of the tree line.

A little girl raised her voice over the boisterous laughter. "Uncle Dengy, tell us about Javensbee?"

Small in stature and just like one of the kids, Dengy jolted backwards in exasperation. "You've heard that so many times."

"But some of us haven't." Their whining pleas echoed through the brush.

"Okay, here goes." They quieted down real fast. "Javensbee was a remarkable planet. It had the most violent weather one could imagine." He hunched over and spoke in whispers. "But this isn't really about the planet. This is about the creature that lived there. Long ago there was this super advanced race. They mastered energy and matter. There was almost nothing they couldn't do. And then they were gone."

"What happened?"

"I'll get to that later. So they selected a planet and began experimenting on ways to control the environment for the benefit of future civilizations. But they were all too good at it. The elements of nature became a life form possessing their abilities; but without the thoughtfulness, compassion and benevolence that came from their many years of experiences. It was called the Songster because it could turn into a windy storm and play beautiful music throughout the numerous mountains and hills. It possessed every element of time and space, light and gravity, fire and water; except it had an evil mind. And you know what happens when there's only evil? The Songster had become an entity made up solely of ego, anger and greed; and these super beings had no way to control it or destroy it."

"Tell us about the Mist?"

"There were four explorers that came to the planet. These super beings gave them immortality and the ability to send the Songster clear out of the galaxy for at least two hundred years. That's how long it would take to make it back for another try. They were known as the Mist. And since they had comparably minimal knowledge, they couldn't divulge any secrets the Songster needed to evolve to its full potential."

"Uncle Dengy, if the Songster was made up of time and space, why didn't it go back in time before the Mist?"

"You're right. Javensbee is by nature time and space. But think of time as a giant web. In order for the Songster to go back in time, he would have to maintain that web throughout all dimensions. It would weaken his integrity as he regressed. Kind of like if you had a cup of juice and kept pouring it out and adding water. Eventually you'd have no juice left. Now on the other hand, the super beings could travel easily through time like you could walk across this camp site. But if they did that, the Songster could hitch a ride without using its own power.

And this was the paradox. They couldn't risk giving Javensbee any more knowledge than it had. So in one great unselfish act they ended their own existence in a single thought and trapped Javensbee forever. He could no longer learn these secrets."

Mother approached the group with a bag of snacks.

"Mom, is the Songster real?"

"It's just a story passed on to me and your uncle."

Another child turned to Dengy. "Do you think it's true?"

"I do, even if my sister doesn't. You see my great, great, great grandfather was told everything personally by the Mist."

"It's true he believed that story", Mother concurred.

A cold wind brushed over the fire and startled them. "Keep going, uncle."

"Two hundred years ago our current governments were on the verge of an historic peace treaty. The meeting place was so secret that the Mist didn't even know about it. And since the last appearance of the Songster was hundreds of years before that, most people didn't even believe it existed. Our ancestor was a guard at that meeting. You know the place in history as Lineesis 249."

"That was an accident."

Dengy extended his lower lip and sucked it back immediately. "That's the official explanation. But our ancestor was there and he told a different story. So all these governments were represented. And then there was a commotion and my ancestor somehow got into the room for a few seconds. He swore that there was a tornado in there that it was killing those dignitaries. The official report was a conduit explosion. But I know it was the Songster."

"Where was the Mist?"

"They arrived too late. They managed to find Javensbee eventually and expelled him out of the galaxy. They have the ability to come together no matter where they are; or so that's what my family's been told."

"Where are they now?"

3

"Nobody knows what they even look like after all these years. We only know that they will never age."

Mother clapped her hands together loudly. "That's enough stories for the night. Let's go to bed."

A choir of disappointment greeted her. They meandered back to the shelters and father joined Dengy and his wife. "You and your Javensbee stories. They're fun, but really?"

"You don't believe in them, sis?"

"I don't know, Dengy. Grandfather believed in them, and his grandfather before that." She looked up at the stars and yawned. "But I think they were just stories to scare and amuse little children."

"But you loved when grandfather told them?"

"I did. But that was a long time ago. We're adults now. Let's get some sleep."

Father smiled devilishly at Dengy. "Your sister tells me you went out on a date with a colleague the other night?"

His face reddened a bit. "Just dinner."

He winked. "Is she a keeper?"

"It was a first date. We work together."

"Your sister tells me you really like her."

"She's nice. Okay?" He tried to change the conversation.

* * * * * * * * * * * * * * * * * * *

The massive scientific institution on the Benarian home world glimmered with silverfish blue surfaces stacked one upon another in sharp edged rectangular designs. The interior was a labyrinth of clear glass corridors emanating soft lighting from hidden sources. Rows of glossy black doors housed the laboratories that produced the breakthroughs society had come to expect.

Dengy and Ale, his diminutive female colleague, were assigned to an insignificant lab rarely frequented by others. Although not as impressive as some facilities, they still had state of the art equipment to perform their tasks. Like most scientists, they moved about their little sterile room in white coats, studying the most recent data. Such was the life of a scientist; hands on experimentation and then hours of tedious analysis.

Ale was seated behind a monitor screen and kept peeking over at Dengy across the room. He'd catch a glimpse of her when she wasn't looking; and then abruptly stare back at his own equipment. Finally he went over to her. "Anything the matter?"

She seemed flustered. "No, why, nothing."

"Come on, Something's on your mind?"

"It's just that we had a good time the other night. At least I thought we did. And you haven't asked me out again."

"I'm sorry. I guess I was nervous."

"Me too. But I had a really good time."

"It was a lot of fun, wasn't it?"

"I tell you what; I'm going to do the asking this time. Dengy, would you like to go out with me tonight?"

"I would."

The head of the department, a stern elder female, barged into the lab. "Dengy, Dr. Tralin would like to see you immediately."

"Really? What did I do?"

"I'm not privileged to that information."

He turned to Ale. "The chief scientist of the institution wants to see me?"

"Don't keep him waiting."

Dr. Tralin's office seemed like an endless journey for an overly concerned Dengy. His shoulders were heavy with doubt as he followed his boss through a maze of corridors and elevators. His thoughts were agitated by scenarios of failure; and worse, dismissal. When they arrived at Tralin's office, his boss excused herself in the foyer and left him there on his own.

Dr. Tralin was at the far end of his lengthy office, facing a wall of monitors. Dengy moved cautiously towards him and then Tralin, a man with gray hair and a narrow salt and pepper goatee, turned around and greeted him enthusiastically. "You must be Dengy of neurological sciences?"

"Yes, sir."

"Sit down, sit down. It has come to my attention that you're working on a new brain wave reconstruction?"

"Yes sir, and I know that it's an already proven science and well established and has a lot of research and…"

"Stop! I'm not here to chastise you. It's true that we haven't had any consequential discoveries in this field for many years, but I am very intrigued on how you're exploring these concepts."

His eyes widened. "You are?"

"Yes. Am I to understand that you believe that a reconstruction process can rebuild original neurons? Andthey may be related to strand reconstruction?"

"Well, yes, I do."

"This kind of experimentation was thought to be improbable. It has been assumed that it might be easier to travel back in time than repair such damage."

"Yes, that has been the conventional wisdom. But it's more like rerouting in order to bridge other areas of the brain; trick the brain into finding a different path. Much like the brain works in order to self repair other damage. It's difficult to explain."

"You don't have to, Dengy. I'm convinced your studies are worth pursuing. I'm recommending we expand your lab and give you additional staff."

"Really? I can't guarantee any results soon."

"You don't have to. Just keep the vision."

"I can use some better equipment; external processing relays. That would help with instant analysis. But I don't need a bigger staff. I work with a scientist named Ale. We can handle everything."

Tralin nodded. "Very well. I'll see to the logistics."

Dengy could hardly restrain his joy while leaving the office. Later that evening he clinked his beverage glass against Ale's at an outdoor restaurant near the city. Not used to drinking much alcohol, he was slightly inebriated. "I can't believe our good fortune. A new lab, new stuff."

Ale sipped her drink as the waiter brought the food still steaming off the plates. She cut a piece of fish, blew on it to cool it down, then put it into her mouth. "You made this all possible. I knew your theories were revolutionary."

"I wouldn't go that far." He slid a chunk of vegetables into his mouth. "But you had a lot to do with it, too." He chewed his food sloppily.

"No Dengy. It's your work. I'm just assisting." She glanced around. "This is a lovely place."

"Think so?" He glommed down another mouthful. "A friend told me about it. Reservations are hard to get."

She reached out to his wrist. "I'm just glad I'm here with you."

He stopped chewing. "I know a good club to go afterwards. Interested?"

"That'd be fun."

"Good. Good. We'll show up late tomorrow. I'm the boss."

Dengy and Ale were transported in a shuttle craft over the foothills of the Benarian suburbs. Sprawling well lit communities were parceled amidst trees and artificial lakes reflecting the twin yellow moons at opposite ends of the horizon. The shuttle nosed downward and followed others towards an octagonal entertainment center on the top of one of the distant mountain peaks. The shuttle delivered them to the front of the club, where dozens of giddy partygoers awaited their turn to enter.

The interior music was muffled, yet laudable as they stood waiting in line. They passed through the well guarded entrance, where a golden escalator led them to the noisy, booming dance floor. On the stage a twelve piece synthesizer band emitted a thumping beat over a sea of gyrating patrons. All around them were radiant flashing lights painting colors across the floor and their clothes.

"This is fabulous!" shouted Ale.

"Told you!"

"You want to dance?"

He slumped sheepishly. "Not really. I'm not good at it."

She tugged him along through the thick crowd. "Come on, it's fun!" She started flailing her arms. "It's easy."

As if he was a wounded animal, Dengy waved his arms and bent his knees. "I feel pretty stupid."

"No, you're doing fine." She slid her fingers between his and pulled him closer. He stepped on her foot, bumped into a dancer behind him and then crashed into Ale's chest. She laughed, held onto his hands and continued to dance. When the music changed and tempo slowed, she could sense he'd had enough. After a few minutes more, she guided him away from the dance floor. "How about a drink?"

"Now I'm for that."

Elbowing his way to the bar, he brought Ale a drink and she followed him out to an open patio with a spectacular view of the mountains. The music was diminished and there were fewer patrons. Ale sniffed the cool air. "This is a wonderful place."

"I wanted it to be special."

"It is. And I couldn't think about being here with anybody other than you."

He gulped down his drink. "I might be a lousy dancer, but I know my clubs."

She cuddled up next to him. "Don't change, Dengy. Don't ever change." She leaned over and kissed him on the mouth.

"Wow. I didn't know it could feel that way."

She rested her head on his shoulder. "Me too."

* *

As awesome and spectacular as it was, this galaxy was just one in a universe of untold numbers. The ordinary cosmic spiral was home to such diversified races, including the ruling Benari and

Makeo. But something else called it home. Out in the silent black void, a bright heated light with a comet's tail sped undeterred towards the furthest regions. It was pure energy formed into a scintillating face with angry gritted teeth and hateful red eyes burning hotter than any star.

In this galaxy the Benari had probably ventured out further than any other species, developing some of the most remote outposts. One such outpost was Eminar 72, a mostly neglected, but still maintained station near a system of cold dead planets. Inside the station a crew member snored loudly from within the confines of his room while his frustrated partner banged his fist on the door. After a few moments of silence, he disassembled a wall panel and yanked out some wires, disrupting the circuitry. The door slid open a few inches and he strained to pull it open completely. He was immediately blasted by a stench of two week old socks and half eaten food. The crewman kept snoring away on his stomach with an arm and leg dangling over the side of the bed.

"Get up, fool!" He remained asleep. "You got to stop drinking so much." He nudged his partner, eventually awaking him.

After a few choking snorts, one eye opened, closed, opened again and stayed open. "What the hell's going on?"

"You've been passed out the first two hours of your shift."

He toppled onto the floor and sat up against the bed. "Like it really matters."

"This morning it does." He threw his shirt at him. "Command's going to call."

"All right, maybe we can get off this dump?" He yawned, farted, and then stumbled down a corridor draped with wires, leaking steam and dried gelatinous material stuck to the walls. The main control room was just as messy as everywhere else. They sat down at their perspective chairs in front of monitor screens, activating the transmission sequence while using their fingers to hastily groom their faces and hair.

Soon a face appeared on the monitors. "I see you two are ready for the galactic cotillion."

"Funny. So how's things in civilized space?"

"Everything's fine here. How about you two?"

"Ready to get off. It's been nine months and we're going crazy. All we've done is tracked an asteroid two months ago."

"There hasn't been that much excitement here either."

"When are the replacements coming?"

His face soured. "I got some bad news. They're not."

They both leaped to their feet. "What!"

"I know you've been there for a long time. But you'll just have to stay put for another month. We just don't have the personnel right now."

"I signed up for eight months."

"Sorry. A supply ship should be there in a few days."

"And we're not going to be on it. That's just great." He terminated the conversation and slammed his fist on the control panel. "Another month."

"No use complaining. Let's get to those environmental controls. Now that we're staying we can't keep putting it off. We won't be able to breathe."

He stood up, resigned to his fate. "You can fix the damn controls. I'm going back to sleep.

Suddenly an array of lights flickered across the control panel. "What's this?"

"I don't know. Looks like an extended sensor reading."

They both sat down at their monitors. "We got something all right. But I don't have a clue of what it is."

"It's powerful enough to trigger an energy surge. And it's not even registering on our long distance sensors."

"Now it is. I'm getting telemetry."

"What is it?"

He shook his head. "I don't know, but its coming fast."

"Crap, I'm starting to get readings on the energy output. If these readings are correct..." His face drained white.

"What is it? A comet? An asteroid?"

"Whatever it is, it's reading more energy than any star I know."

He punched at a few controls. "This is no comet. It's moving too fast. And here's the bad news, it's heading right for us."

His partner covered his mouth. "It's going to hit us!"

"Will the shields hold?"

He gazed over at him in disbelief. "Can the shields stop a star?"

"I'm going to activate the main monitor. I've got a visual."

On the screen was a white hot object expanding in width as it approached the station. Blinded with fingers gripped tightly onto the edge of the console, fear overcame them in anticipation of the collision. The object filled the screen, illuminating the entire control room. Preparing to die and wetting their pants, they reared back and braced for impact. Eyes shut tight, fingers molded to the console; the object directly hit them without causing any damage. The silence jolted them out of paralysis.

Dumbfounded, they stared at each other. "What happened?"

Rigid and unable to move, their heads slowly swiveled around to peek at the back of the room where a strikingly handsome humanoid with watery green eyes, perfectly coifed black hair, gray pants and red vest stood passively with arms crossed. He just loomed at them with barely a smile and it took them a couple seconds to respond.

"Who the hell are you?"

Arms still crossed, he began to relax his posture. "Who or what I am is of no concern of yours."

"Did you just see what happened? All of us should have been killed."

"Tell me, who rules this galaxy now?"

"Listen pal, I don't know who you are or what you want. But we just had survived a light coming at us with tremendous readings and then disappear."

11

"Again I ask, who rules this galaxy?"

Puzzled, one of them stood up. "The Benari and Makeo are in charge, if that's what you mean. And right now you're trespassing on a Benarian station."

"Are you at war?"

The other stood. "Where have you been? We've been at peace for ninety years."

The stranger's head dropped. "Then I was not succesful."

"So where's your vessel? We didn't detect you."

He snickered quietly. "Vessel? How primitive." He meandered over to a protruding bulkhead and stroked the surface erotically. "It's good to feel solid mass. Do you realize how long it has been? Such emptiness."

The crewman wearily inched his way towards a wall cabinet. "You're going to have to leave now."

"Leave?" He leaned against the bulkhead and continued stroking it. "I've just arrived."

The crewman removed a small laser pistol from the cabinet and aimed it at him. "We're going to have to ask you to stay in one of our storage areas until our supply ship comes. They can decide what to do with you."

He closed his eyes, pressed his body against the bulkhead and then pushed himself away. "You think that little toy can persuade me?"

"Just cooperate for your own good." The crewman began to tremble. He painfully winced and dropped the pistol on the ground. It became red hot, then white, and then melted into the floorboard. "What do you want from us?" the other asked.

"Want? I want nothing from you. You happen to be the first beings I encountered. And for that, I am truly sorry."

"What are you going to do to us?"

His eyes drifted from side to side. "You have a very primitive plasma reactor."

"Why do you say that?"

"What would happen if it were to come into contact with a slightly corrosive substance?"

"It would kill us all."

The stranger smiled and his humanoid body filled up with a churning, raging torrent of blue and red liquid. He raised his arms high above his head and dropped through the floor without a single drop of residue left behind.

* *

Dengy sat across from Dr. Tralin in his office. Tralin was perusing through some recent work. "Interesting."

"You have to understand that I'm just getting use to the equipment."

"I wasn't criticizing you, Dengy."

"I just don't want you to have too high of expectations. We're a long way off for actual trials."

He peered over his desk. "Dengy, you appear slightly nervous, unsettled. I know your wedding is next week. Perhaps you and Ale should take some time off?"

"That's not necessary. I am distracted. But it's because my work is in such preliminary stages."

"But it's promising."

"The equipment has made a big difference. We're getting rapid information. That could lead to results much sooner."

"Still, I want you to concentrate on your wedding."

"Ale's doing most of the arrangements."

"After you're married, you may find it awkward to work together. But we've had married couples that have coped quite well."

"I've thought about it. But I can't think of anyone else I want to be with."

Dr. Tralin's assistant barged into the room. "Check your monitor. There's been an accident. They're having a news conference."

Dengy swung around to the back of his desk and they watched the transmission. "I'm here with the first Agitate of the Eminar quadrant. "What do you know so far?"

"We know a supply ship arrived approximately two hours ago at Eminar 72, a remote outpost. Upon arrival they found the outpost to be completely destroyed. We found debris, but very small pieces. It has been determined to be an explosion, but the cause is unknown. We have confiscated two of the largest pieces of the outer hull that are approximately about four feet in length and width."

"Were there any survivors?"

"Unfortunately the two crew members are presumed dead. It is still our hope that somehow they would have been forewarned and made it to safety. But as of now, we've had no contact from them. Their families have been notified."

"Could it have been a hostile attack?"

"As you know, Eminar 72 is a very remote outpost in a region that is fairly unprotected. As of now we have no evidence it was attacked. There were no ships in the area, nor any sign of warp signatures. It is important to note that the station was protected by shielding and the crew should have had some kind of warning. But remember this investigation is still in its preliminary stages and we are currently conducting search and rescue."

"Will you have an analysis of the debris soon?"

"I can't answer that definitively. But I assure you the tests will be revealed at the earliest possible moment."

Dr. Tralin ended the transmission. "How terrible."

Dengy was saddened. "I can't remember when anything like that has happened." He saw that Tralin seemed preoccupied. "Is there something wrong?"

"No. No, Dengy. That sector is so remote. Who knows what kind of things can happen out there."

Several days later Dengy's wedding would take place on a planet known for its dynamic waterfalls at every venue. The outdoor assembly was perched high upon a hillside with caged birds encompassing a flowery garden that made the bride and groom the envy of all those in attendance. The guests arrived on the landing port and were ushered to their seats. After a multitude of droning voices, they became silent when the couple showed up hand in hand.

Trembling and anxious, Dengy winked at his niece in the front row, who sat enthralled next to her mother. The ceremony lasted a short time with concurrent vows written and recited by each. After the marriage pronouncement, Ale's eyes dreamily gazed into his and they kissed and were accompanied by a healthy applause from the excited guests. The birds were finally released and flew off erratically into different directions.

The reception followed indoors, where the tables surrounded an elegant twenty foot marble and quartz centerpiece with textured flowers from other worlds. Dengy's sister was the first to rise and propose a toast to her brother and new wife. "I only wish my parents could be here to see this fantastic day. It boggles the mind when my little brother, who studied science every minute of the day and night, could end up with such a catch."

Dr. Tralin stood up and toasted the couple. "It's just fortunate that both bride and groom work for the same boss. And I must say that it's an honor to attend such a delightful event. I suppose it may be more difficult now to decide who to listen to at work in the future." They all chuckled politely. "But I assure you it will be Ale."

Dengy's niece stood up. "I'm also glad my uncle got married. I love my new aunt. But I'm also a little worried."

"Why", asked Dengy.

"You might not tell me those stories anymore."

He placed his arm around her. "Course I will."

Her father stood up and loudly announced, "Let's get this party going!"

The remainder of the day consisted of guests gorging on appetizers, drinking plenty of liquor and dancing exuberantly. Hours later the couple boarded a shuttle and embarked on their honeymoon. While the party resumed unabated for many hours to come, Dengy and Ale were dropped off at a tropical island resort with reservations on the beach in a primitive hut with all the modern conveniences.

"We're finally here"

Ale luxuriated in the mild ocean breezes. "It's perfect, Dengy." She took his hand. "I couldn't think of a better place."

His eyebrows wiggled. "We should go inside."

Ale excused herself while Dengy loitered on the deck and listened to the squawking sea birds and gentle swells lapping at the water's edge. He squinted into the sunlight and turned to see his bring draped in a flowery sarong. He became excited when she led him into the bedroom and aggressively pushed him down on the mattress. She kissed him and he gladly succumbed to her; enjoying lovemaking for the hours to come.

Later that evening they called for room service and ordered a plate of island snacks and exotic wine. "Trying to get me drunk, huh?"

"Oh, I think we're past that."

"We're really married, can you believe it. It's like a dream. I don't think I ever want to go back to work."

He kissed her. "We don't have to think about that now."

* *

Javensbee streaked through open space in the form of a comet followed by a razor thin tail. He decelerated and slowly morphed into splintery chips of cohesive metal particles. Part energy, part metal; the chips annealed to one another, configuring into a solid, indistinguishable mass. The metal soon twisted into the frame of a space vessel as he entered into Makeo territory.

Unlike the Benarian architecture, Makeo space ports and cities were brightly painted and lacked rigid angles. There were spherical shapes connected to tubular corridors branching off into upwardly sweeping extremities that wound through a lattice of windowless structures. They were a dominant military power and proudly showed off their stubby war vessels, each with rippled hulls sporting extravagant protrusions.

Javensbee slowed considerably as he approached the outskirts of the Makeo solar system and was immediately intercepted by two ships. "Galconian vessel, state your purpose?"

"I'm a trader, here to see General Hecor."

There was silence, and then a response. "That is not possible without prior authorization. Please follow us to command."

"That will be acceptable."

Javensbee followed the escort into the bowels of the Makeo infrastructure. They speedily ducked under and over misshapen red, yellow and blue buildings, spheres, corridors and towering spindles. All the colorful surfaces were illuminated and shadowed by a giant orange star powering the entire system. A large door opened in a nearby sphere and Javensbee was guided into a landing dock where a contingent of guards awaited.

The Makeo were a much different species than the Benari. Although humanoid, their bodies were short, arms long and their faces stretched out horizontally with oversized heads. They were hairless and had pointed chins of various lengths; sometimes sticking out as much as six inches.

Javensbee emerged from his craft and was marched towards an open door at the end of the dock. He was asked to be seated and soon a Makeo officer walked up to him. "My name is Lieutenant Fecan. I understand you wish to see General Hecor."

"My name is Oribud of Galcon. I'm a trader and I may have something of importance for the general."

He stared insolently. "The general is supreme commander of all our forces. It is highly unlikely you would receive an audience with him."

"I'm well aware of that. However, I think you'd be wise to alert him."

"Tell me your message and I will bring it to him."

"With all due respect, Lieutenant, you are just the hired help."

Fecan's face widened with rage. "I could have you arrested for that comment."

Javensbee responded in a more conciliatory tone. "Forgive me, Lieutenant. I was a bit brash. I must speak to General Hecor." He removed a small cubical device from his coat pocket. "Please take this to your scientists."

Fecan tumbled it between his fingers. "What is it?"

"It's a new energy source. I'm certain your scientists will be intrigued." He removed another device from his coat. "Use this to contact me once General Hecor gets the report from your scientists."

Fecan smugly pointed at his guards. "Show our friend here out of our space."

"Thank you, Lieutenant. Until an opportune time."

Fecan watched the guards escort him away and then pulled another officer over to him. "Follow him. I want to know where he goes."

Javensbee steered away from the Makeo system with three cloaked ships following behind him. He was amused at their attempt, but remained on a light speed course towards Galcon space. He maneuvered past five planets in a binary star system and settled into orbit around the sixth. The Makeo ships kept tracking him until his ship darted downward through the atmosphere and vanished from their sensors.

"What happened? Where'd he go?"

"Uncertain, sir. I'm not reading any energy signatures on the planet. No life forms of any kind."

"That can't be. Initialize another sweep. The last thing we want to do is explain to Fecan that we lost him."

Galcon space was originally a Makeo territory, but had been under Benari control for the last four hundred years. After the most recent peace treaty ninety years ago it had once again been annexed by the Makeo. It was just one of many provinces that changed leadership through a series of painful compromises. Although most Galconians were content with Makeo administrative oversight, there was a faction that preferred the Benarian government.

In the distant region of Galcon space the Makeo maintained several outposts, each with compliments of two hundred personnel. Typical of Makeo military bases, their peak efficiency was the envy of all societies. The surfaces were bright lime green with three elliptical spheres connected by protruding corridors. Inside the station the crew worked tirelessly on regularly scheduled shifts, unaware of the visitor that had just invaded their solitude.

Javensbee stealthily traveled through the interior bulkheads, expanding them as he undulated like a worm through the metal. He whipped around corners, over ceilings and through hallways, finally bursting out and landing on the deck as a fully formed Makeo crew member. Arms almost dragging on the floor, he met another crew member that was on her way to work her shift. Without speaking, he touched her shoulder and half her body dissolved to the floor in a lump of dissolved flesh. He casually strolled to the main fusion reactor room unnoticed by the busy crew. He stood in front of the giant oscillating reactor and was surprised by an officer. "You there, don't just stand around. I need a calibration."

Without responding, Javensbee raised his arms high over his head and caused the reactor to reverberate at a higher frequency. Panicked, the officer and his crew tried to compensate for the overload, but had no effect. Seconds later the reactor, along with entire station, exploded into thousands of outwardly projected particles. Javensbee simply turned into a streak of energy and flew away from the molten debris.

General Hecor, adorned in packs of military ribbons and medals, paced around excitedly upon receiving the news of the doomed outpost. A group of subordinate officers tried calming him down, but he kept waving those long arms in near hysteria.

Lieutenant Fecan entered the room. "Excuse me, General, Oribud of Galcon is waiting to see you."

"Who?"

"You gave orders to notify you when the Galcon trader was here."

"Oh yes, send him in immediately."

Javensbee strutted into the room. "General Hecor, I presume?"

"We've just had a horrible accident in Galcon space."

"I heard about it."

Hecor set the cube down on a table top. "You gave this to my Lieutenant?"

"I take it you've had it analyzed?"

"My scientists have concluded there is more energy in this cube than the entire outpost that exploded. The question is... how?"

"General, there are some secrets that I wish to keep to myself. However, this source of energy in readily available to me."

"So what do you want, Oribud?"

"General, I am a loyal Galcon citizen. My forefathers were loyal to the Makeo centuries ago. I sense there is a movement to divest and return to Benari rule. This would be abhorrent to me."

"Oribud, I too am loyal to my government. And what I think about this matter is not my concern. It is left to the civilian government to make such decisions. We are a democracy. So getting back to this energy source, are you willing to discuss some kind of business arrangement?"

"I have a weapon, General Hecor. One like no other weapon in this galaxy. It utilizes this power source and the one who controls it, has control of everything. I assure you that the Makeo and the Benari have no such weapon in their arsenals."

"And what would we do with such a weapon?"

Javensbee laughed. "An irrelevant question. I see you don't

believe me. But I have the weapon and I could demonstrate it for you."

"We don't register any kind of weapon on your ship?"

"None the less, it is there. My proposal is simple. You equip an insignificant moon in a system of your choosing and protect it with your most advanced shielding. I will show you what my weapon can do."

"I'm certain we can find such a moon. But this better not be a waste of my time."

"I assure you, this is not a waste of your time. But there is one thing. I suggest you find a satellite that will not affect the gravitational structure of a nearby planetary system."

Hecor burst out laughing. "You must have some confidence in your weapon. And judging by the energy source in this cube, I'd say you might have good reason."

"Then it's your move."

"I'd say a moon in the Qiuorin system should suffice. You may give Fecan the information necessary to load your weapon on one of our vessels."

"You will not be disappointed, General."

Javensbee's weapon was a six foot long missile at least five inches in diameter. The outer shell was a burnished gold color and the Makeo instruments were unable to scan its contents. This frustrated the ordinance officer, who was utterly mystified as Javensbee directed its relocation into a medium sized Makeo crusier

General Hecor boarded the cruiser and ordered the departure. "Our destination is about an hour's distance from here."

"This is a great day for you, General. Perhaps one day all your ships will have my weapons on them."

"Your presumption is noted, Oribud. But I've seen these things not turn out the way they were intended."

All five planets of the selected solar system were lifeless and void of any atmosphere. One such sphere had a gray pocked moon that was on an elliptical orbit around its mother planet.

They erected a mobile shield device comprised of two vertical crescent shaped metallic structures one mile equidistant from each other. Between the structures flowed a class 14 energy shield; the most powerful repelling force in the Makeo inventory.

"So we are, Oribud. Let's see what you got?"

"General, we might be too close."

He chuckled, pointing at the moon. "We're ten thousand miles away."

"I'd make it twenty."

His chin wiggled amusingly. "All right, do as he says."

Javensbee pulled out a device from his pocket and entered a sequence of numbers. "The weapon is now under your control, General."

Hecor ordered the missile to be aimed directly at the middle area between the shields. To his astonishment, the missile easily penetrated the shield and proceeded towards the moon's surface. It exploded upon impact, blowing a five hundred foot crater of rock and dust into space; some of the bigger chunks grazing past their vessel. The moon had been dislodged from orbit and the gravitational forces began to rip it apart until it completely lost its form. To Hecor's disbelief, the rest of the rocky debris just hung out there motionless in the midst of space. His tongue fell out of his mouth. "What did we just see?"

"The future, General."

"This weapon is like nothing I've ever seen; or imagined. How does it work? Where does this science come from?"

"So many questions, General. And I will answer them in time. But understand this. There is no other weapon in its class."

"I believe you. And the price for such a weapon?"

"That's a delicate matter. I have considered payment options. But they are probably not what you'd expect. As I said before, I am a loyal Galcon of the old order. There may come a time when a weapon like this could be given to the right buyer."

"I too share some of your loyalties. But as I have said before, we are a civilian government. I will have to speak to my President and the Council."

"There is one more favor. You sent your officers to track me. Please don't do that again. I will look elsewhere for a buyer."

"It will not happen again. I assure you."

The Council chamber was located in the heart of the Makeo orbiting structures in the center of the system. It was a flattened disc shape with a phosphorescent red exterior and thousands of yellow metallic tentacles extending outward in every direction. The President and twenty Council members were seated in circular fashion in the middle of amphitheatre seating.

General Hecor and Lieutenant Fecan were the only two in the room. The Council had just reviewed the moon's destruction and the members were as amazed as Hecor at the monumental destruction.

The distinguished elder female President tapped her long boney finger on the table. "And you say the missile was small?"

"Yes, Madam President. There was nothing extraordinary about it."

She cupped her hand over her mouth, and then exhaled a prolonged breath. "This is nothing short of a weapon of mass destruction. This weapon can not be justified in today's civilized society."

"I'm not suggesting we keep it from the Benari. It just seems irresponsible not to explore its possibilities."

A Council member interrupted. "General Hecor may be correct. We must assume that Oribud may seek another buyer

She stood up authoritatively. "That may be true. But we can not assume this Galcon trader would not use it himself."

"He hasn't so far."

"That's a good point, General. But I believe a weapon of this kind could destabilize the peace. We have a strong alliance with the Benari."

"That is true, Madam President. And I wouldn't suggest

harming that relationship. If we were to acquire this weapon, it would be for defensive purposes."

"Be careful, General. You are dangerously close to suggesting a holocaust."

He bowed his head. "I apologize for my presumption. I would just hope that you and the Council would discuss the situation."

TWO

DR. TRALIN'S ESTATE ON THE Benarian home world was spectacular, befitting one of their greatest scientists. It sat atop a sheer cliff overlooking a valley as green as nature could produce. The house was layers upon layers of sharp angled pale blue facades that glimmered in the late afternoon. Triangular decks overhung the backyard precipice and a retractable roof half way exposed the receding sunlight. A powerful river cut through the valley floor; its source coming from a rock pounding waterfall not far from the house.

Dr. Tralin sat on his couch and sipped an alcoholic beverage made from sweet fruit he'd grown on the estate. He reviewed his day's work on a full walled monitor across the living room, soothed by fragrant winds that carried across his nostrils from an open patio. A few native birds landed on the balcony rail as he wandered outside to enjoy the last light of day.

He held onto to the rail, closed then opened his eyes as he sniffed the freshest air imaginable while a thinly laced moistened breeze tickled his face from an almost cloudless sky. Each side of the valley had tremendous cliffs and the ever present river lured him into a steady trance. And then he was distracted; though not much of a distraction at first. He could swear the reddish purple horizon began to form clouds instantly. He figured it must have been an illusion, yet they persisted and seem to become more organized.

Puzzled, he cocked his head to the right and intensely clutched the rail. Other clouds began to form nearer to his house; but they didn't appear natural. They moved in such a path to shadow the river, becoming thicker and darker high above the valley floor. The soft wind began to increase, ruffling his gray hair and frightening the rest of the birds away. Though he didn't understand what was happening, he certainly felt uneasy.

Jolts of lightening sparked across brownish red clouds and blowing gusts of wind swirled with patches of leaves and twigs. Some of the debris deposited on his balcony while thunderous claps reverberated inside the clouds. He could barely make out a small disturbance within the approaching storm; one that was even darker and twisting faster to form a disorganized tornado.

Tralin released his grip on the balcony rail and began to back away. The storm grew more ominous and tightened as to resemble a raging tornado funnel at least twenty feet tall. He could see bands of brighter red twisting around the funnel, which now shrunk in size as it approached the balcony. Tralin backed up to the door as it hovered near the rail and then over the balcony and into the house. Though furious, it didn't knock over any furniture or cause destruction. It just hovered in the center of the living room, slightly warbling from side to side.

Tralin was more curious than frightened. The tornado then slightly decreased in velocity and changed into a humanoid figure; still violently twirling in mass. The revolutions subsided and the once undefined humanoid figure spun to a sudden stop. Tralin could hardly believe what had materialized in the room. "Javensbee…"

"Hello, Dr. Tralin. That is the name you are going by these days? The last time we met you were a botanist, I believe."

Tralin encircled him guardedly. "It has been many years."

Javensbee's piercing green eyes squinted disappointedly. "To my great displeasure, the Benari and Makeo were able to make peace."

"That peace wouldn't have taken so long if we had found you earlier."

Javensbee observed every corner of the living room. "You've done quite well for yourself. An esteemed position, luxurious home."

"I've helped a lot of people, if that's what you mean? Something you would not know about."

He waved his finger contemptibly. "Now, now, Dr. Tralin. Let's not get personal. What you're really thinking is why I've announced myself so boldly to you."

"It is not like you, Javensbee. You usually hide like a coward. Of course you must know I will summon the Mist?"

He leaped around the room enthusiastically. "I do, I do! And that's the best thing about this. I know something that you don't know. Something fantastic. So, go ahead and call the Mist."

Puzzled, Tralin extended his arm and a purplish glow emanated from his palm.

"Something wrong?"

He gazed seriously at his hand. The glow persisted, but there was no reaction. "I don't understand this."

"Not getting an answer, huh? And I know why. And I can't wait for you to find out. I can't wait."

He clenched his fist. "So, it appears we're powerless."

"And I am the only one that knows why."

"Somehow you have found a way to neutralize us."

"No, that's the beauty of it. I did nothing. But I am the only one that knows why."

Tralin plopped down on the couch. "Have you come to destroy the galaxy?"

"Ahh, so you're thinking that the Mist will be the only ones that will survive. After all, I still can't destroy you. We are immortal."

"Tell me Javensbee, are you responsible for those outposts?"

"Yes…and yet you still look confused."

"Forgive me, but I am. Here you are without any adversaries and the citizens of the galaxy are still alive."

He strolled behind the couch, dragging his finger across the top lip. "I have other objectives this time. I will reveal them to you at the proper time."

"I know it has to involve war."

"Correct. I'm offering the Makeo a weapon that can destroy entire solar systems."

"I know of no such weapon."

He pranced around the room rapturously. "You're right, you're right! You see, I am the weapon. A few holographic deceptions and I'm free to take the shape of a devastating missile."

"Why are you telling me all this?"

"I have my reasons. This Mist has been a fable for two thousand years. Now there is no reason to hide your identity. You can shout my arrival on the top of the mountains. The game is over and we both know it."

"I suppose you're going to ransack my residence now?"

Javensbee extended both arms straight out, turned back into a raging tornado, lifted off the floor, flew over to a small end table between a couch and chair and collapsed it into several pieces. He vanished, leaving other parts of the living room undisturbed. Tralin stood there silently, and then ran over to his desk computer. He immediately contacted a fury creature with four eyes and six arms. "I must speak to Talisa Caru."

"Dr. Tralin, that may be difficult. She is engaged as a mercenary soldier in the Mulor System. Our contacts have been minimal."

"It's very important. Can you send her a message?"

"I will try at the earliest opportunity."

He terminated the transmission and contacted a towering silicon based entity without any detectable facial features. "I'm trying to get a hold of Golbot of Herenia. My name is Dr. Tralin."

"Golbot has been unavailable for these three months. We believe his last position was in the Yirerian Nebula."

"I must find him."

"I understand. Treasure hunters are hard to find, Dr. Tralin. They rarely divulge their itinerary. Are you a business acquaintance?"

"In a way. If you do hear from him, please tell him I need to speak with him." Tralin contacted another species, a cerebral humanoid woman. "Hello, Dr. Wison. It has been many years."

"It has."

"I need to speak to Dr. Ceylar."

"That may be a problem. My last conversation with him was three years ago. He seems to have made himself unavailable."

"I'm sorry to hear that. The last thing I heard was that you and he were on a project together."

"Our alliance was unsuccessful. He chose another direction."

"If you should hear from him, please have him contact me."

"I will do so."

Tralin rose from his desk and a realization of helplessness smacked his head as if he were hit by a rock. The tremendous burden set upon him and the Mist was almost too much to bear as they were apparently unable to stop their adversary from unimaginable destruction. He was frustrated, confused and alone; unable to contact the others. He just walked out to the balcony, listened to the waterfall and observed the last strip of purplish red light flicker over the horizon.

* ** * *

Eminar space was a vast territory once ruled by the Makeo, but has been since governed by the Benari. Much like Galcon space had to readjust to the Makeo, those of the Eminar quadrant had to do so for the Benari. Although space station 60 was not as distant as the recently destroyed Eminar 72, it was still considered remote. It had a crew of four Benari and had more interior levels than Eminar 72. A supply ship had just left the docking area and the crew was busy storing the new food and equipment.

"Get that damn plate lifter over here!"

"I can't help it if the balancer is defective."

"Complain, complain. The sooner we get this stuff away, the sooner we can call it quits."

"Yes, sir."

The Benarian foreman took the elevator up to the main control center, where another crew member was at the monitor. "Signal command that we received the supplies. Everything's accounted for." He then smiled at the crew member. "We got that vetiron steak meat I ordered."

"Eating good tonight."

The console began to light up. "What's this?"

The foreman leaned over him. "Looks like long range sensors detect Makeo."

"I think I can get a visual."

A diminutive Makeo vessel with a stubby bow filled the monitor screen. "Makeo vessel, state your business?"

"We got a little present for you."

Twin laser beams impacted the outer shields, shaking the crew to the floor. "Shields are down! Shields are down!"

The foreman leaped up and activated a distress call. "We're under attack from the Mak…"

The outpost exploded into a million shards of metal that drifted outward in every direction and then halted in place to form a scattered debris field. The Makeo vessel morphed back into Javensbee's comet and sped away into the emptiness.

General Hecor was just finishing a bowl full of live rodents when Lieutenant Fecan interrupted his solitude. "General, we've just intercepted a message to the Benarian high command."

He choked down a slithering tail. "So what did it say, Fecan?"

"Eminar 60 may have been destroyed."

"Damn."

"There weren't any specifics, but they did receive a partial message. They think it sounded like mak...or even Makeo."

"We don't have anybody out there."

"No, not presently."

He chewed the last morsel. "All we can do is sit back and wait for them to react. But it doesn't look good for us."

Hours passed by before the first rescue crew arrived at Eminar 60. They found complete destruction, but were unable to determine the cause or find any residual proof of an attack. Admiral Jarret, Hecor's Benarian counterpart, soon contacted the general at Makeo military command. "General, it appears we may have a problem."

"We heard about your outpost. My condolences."

"We're still in the preliminary stages of investigation. But this is the second outpost destroyed and we must now assume the possibility of a hostile attack."

"I agree."

"There's one more thing, Hecor. We received a message that sounded like it could have been Makeo."

"I can assure you our nearest vessel was five light years away. In any case I will give permission for your command to review all Makeo military operations in that area."

"That would be more than sufficient. General Hecor, I assure you that we do not believe the Makeo is responsible for any of the outpost attacks."

"I appreciate that."

"Has there been any progress on your investigations?"

"Not as yet."

The transmission ended and Lieutenant Fecan saluted. "If there is anything else, by your leave?" He started walking away, and then turned around. "Excuse me, General. Do you believe him?"

"Whether I believe him or not, he did offer his operational files."

∗ ∗

Dengy and Ale had just purchased a new residence on an orbiting space station near their home world. It was an ideal location for those of middle class stature and had three bedrooms, a modest living room and kitchen, and a small balcony shielded from the outside elements.

One evening when the station was turned away from the planet and overlooking a myriad of stars, the couple argued about a green and yellow plant in the corner of the balcony. "I would have preferred something with flowers", Dengy asserted.

"There are flowers all over the house. This is a rare plant."

"Yeah, but it's kind of scraggily."

"It should grow out, I think."

"We'll be in our next house by then."

He noticed her distraction. "Dengy, speaking about our next house; and our future. I know we're busy scientists, but…"

"What's on your mind?"

"I was talking to your sister the other day, and…"

"This is not like you. Just tell me?"

She placed both palms on the table top. "I know we're career orientated, but I think we should talk about a family."

He bolted upright in his chair and his expression turned gloomy. "Sure."

"You don't sound positive. Kind of disappointed."

"No. I mean, we have to think about it."

"This means a lot to me, Dengy. How much thinking do you need?"

He smiled. "Of course I want to have a family one day."

She stood up irritated. "Don't you want somebody other than me to listen to those stories of yours? Like your own kids."

"I look forward to the day we have children. Yes, the project is taking all our time now. But it won't always be that way."

"Just don't take too long."

"Have a little patience, Ale. Everything's moving so fast"

* *

The Makeo space station in the Niero colony was once under Benari rule. It was larger than most outposts and was situated above a gaseous planet encircled by red and white storm bands wrapped around its surface. In typical Makeo architectural the structure had a series of colorful ovular sections with a contingency of at least fifty crew members. An active entry port was crowded with vessels arriving and departing on regular schedules. There was a distant mother star and several other planets, but the station's orbit was mostly influenced by the nearby gaseous planet.

Inside the main control center the Makeo crew coordinated the mining operations for the other solid planets. Since the region was considered valuable in minerals, the station had formidable defenses. The crew was particularly anxious because a government inspector was reviewing procedures with the station commander. "I must say, your operation is much more involved than I previously thought."

"We keep very busy with three shifts."

He snidely placed his calculator in his pocket. "And yet I find gross mismanagement."

Perturbed, the commander waved his long arms. "You haven't even inspected a tenth of the station and have come to that conclusion?"

"True. But a review of your daily inventory has suggested there is room for improvement."

"We are operating in deep space, inspector. There are logistical problems out here."

He smirked. "Just because you are out here does not excuse a pitiful lack of production."

"I would hardly call it pitiful."

"I have estimated by adding a fourth shift, flexibly alternated, you could increase production by ten per cent."

"Yes, but that would cause dissention among the employees."

"Employees? That is your concern? I'm certain we could recruit a whole new crew that would appreciate the benefits of this work."

The commander was about to lose his temper when a crew member shouted out from behind a console. "An urgent message's coming in."

"What?"

"It appears to be a Benarian shuttle. It's taken heavy damage. I'm reading one life sign. Very faint."

"Beam him directly to the infirmary. Get a tractor on that shuttle." He turned to the inspector. "You'll have to excuse me."

The commander arrived in the medical unit where the doctor was treating a severely burned male Benarian. "I don't think he's going to survive."

"Can I speak to him?"

"Yes. He's conscious."

The commander leaned over and quietly spoke to him. "What happened?"

"Warning", he moaned. "Benarian attack squadron."

"Why did they attack you?"

The man died. The Commander then communicated with his control room officer. "Scan for long range ships!"

He hustled out of the room and the doctor activated a storage chamber to secure the corpse; which vanished once inside. The Commander joined his second in command who had just ordered continual sweeps of the sector. Without any target identification, the Commander called for a secondary alert status; but then changed his mind and ordered a full red alert. No sooner did he give the order when five Benarian attack vessels showed up on the long range sensors. Alarms then rang out all over the station.

"Benarian vessels, state your purpose?"

Unresponsive to hails, the Commander restrained his crew from firing their weapons. One of the Benarian vessels broke formation and took position in front of the others. At speeds of 200,000 miles per hour, they kept in a tight formation at first and then began to spread out while reducing speeds by half. The lead vessel fired three laser beams at the middle section of the station and caused minor damage.

"Stop or we'll return weapon's fire!"

"They're responding."

"Makeo station, surrender in the name of the Benarian Empire."

The Commander slammed his fist on the console. "Send a message to base we're under attack!"

"Unable, sir. They're jamming our frequencies."

"They can't do it. Override it!"

"No effect. They must have our codes."

The Benari squadron circled the station complex in formation and then separated and cruised around the circumference.

"Okay they want a fight, give them everything we got."

"Right away, sir."

One of the Benari vessels fired at the shields and eliminated the Makeo defenses in one burst. The other ships gathered near the middle section and fired a volley of missiles at the outer shell, which exploded outwards, killing the Commander and the rest of the crew immediately. The Benari vessels concentrated their fire on one of the outer sections and disintegrated it into shards of heated metal. The crew of the remaining section was unable to fire weapons and prepared for their demise when all the vessels disappeared.

"Where'd they go!"

There was silence for a moment and then Javensbee appeared in the control room. He was immediately lasered by a Makeo crew member, but it passed through him. He casually walked over to a bulkhead and pressed his hand against it. The bulkhead exploded outwardly and the vacuum of space sucked out most of the crew. As they drifted away, Javensbee morphed into a tornado and swirled from room to room; blowing out huge chunks of wall and expelling crew members out into space. Pleased with his efforts, he changed back into a comet and zipped off into the darkness.

It wasn't long after that the first rescue ships arrived at the crumbled station. An order was immediately given halt all mining operations and to evacuate all non essential personnel off the other planets. Reinforcements were sent to guard the system and a full investigation proceeded.

Lieutenant Fecan entered Hecor's office with a sour expression. "General, I'm sorry to report that there were no survivors on the station."

"And the miners?"

"All accounted for."

"This is no coincidence. We are being targeted."

Fecan set a small device down on Hecor's desk. "There's something you must see. This event was a well planned assault."

"I knew it."

"What you're viewing on your monitor is from one of our long range sensors on one of the moons."

"Those are Benari attack vessels!"

"Yes, they are."

"Then it's war."

"Apparently the Makeo crew were unable to send out a distress call. The Benari must have had some kind of inhibitor."

"So they've been quietly upgrading their military. I'm going to take this to the President immediately."

Fecan's fingers twitched. "General, are you going to advise the council to seek the Galcon trader, Oribud?"

"Let's not be presumptuous, Lieutenant. If this is truly war, then I believe all means necessary to protect our civilians will be considered."

The President and her council sat stoically in the rounded chamber as general Hecor presented the dire facts. They all realized that ninety years of peace was jeopardized and the possibility of war now existed. There was unanimous agreement that the Makeo citizens would not be notified until a complete investigation was undertaken.

"Madam President, it is obvious that the Benari have been planning this for a long time."

"That may be, General Hecor. But I'm not prepared to make any rash accusations before we know all the facts. It is not the time to abandon all diplomacy with a species we've been at peace with."

"Peace is one thing. But I'm willing to bet that two of our military bases were deliberately attacked by the Benari. Perhaps in response to Eminar."

"I will confer with the Benarian Chancellor. If his answers not satisfactory, then our governments may have a confrontation."

Hecor pranced away from the curved table, waving his arms. "What is he going to say, sorry we just wanted to take over the galaxy?"

"General, please keep your place. The council has the authority to make those decisions, not you."

"Very well. But our citizens will eventually demand a full accounting." He charged out of the room without excusing himself.

The President turned to her council. "We are in a difficult position. To the fact we have damnable evidence is obvious. But is that evidence what it seems to be? I must truly tell you I do not believe that the Benari want war. This could be faction that wants to discredit the Benari.

"Madam President, do you wish me to relay the evidence to the Benari Chancellor?"

"Yes. Right away. We'll give them a little time to digest the facts and then we'll wait for their response."

"Might this give them an opportunity to strike us first?"

"If we really are on the brink of war, the attack would have already begun. We must handle this with extreme delicacy."

Time passed by excruciatingly and then the Chancellor appeared on the large monitor screen. "Madam President, the Benari council has received your evidence and is most disturbed by its implication. Before we discuss this, I want to send my condolences for your loss of life and assure you that this was not a Benari operation."

"Of course I believe you, Chancellor. But there are many in my government and military that will not. Perhaps these vessels were stolen?"

"The problem, Madam President, is that stolen Benari vessels would have immediately come to our attention."

"I appreciate any cooperation, but I must be accountable to the opposition. I think it best that we suspend trade in this sector for the time being. If that indicates skepticism on my part, I make no apologies for that."

"I understand. I would feel the same way. I have my opposition parties as well who believe the Eminar explosions were not accidental."

"One thing we must keep in perspective, Chancellor. Future attacks could damage our alliance beyond containment."

"There's another issue I think should be addressed. Perhaps our military operations should become more transparent."

"I agree with your assessment. This kind of trust should go a long way to soothe those with opposing views and avoid war."

"On behalf of my government, again our deepest sympathies. Benari Chancellor, ending transmission."

The Benari council then shouted their disapproval. One Minister raised an index finger high in the air. "The Makeo practically accused us of sedition!"

"We can't just hand over our military secrets."

The Chancellor seemed circumspect. "We are not facing a trivial dispute. War with the Makeo would be devastating and possibly genocidal. If a few gestures of faith can avert war, then is it not worth it?"

"The Chancellor is correct. Diplomacy is our only option. Let's not forget that it was a Makeo station and these pictures of our war vessels attacking are not to be dismissed outright."

"I'm going to order a full military investigation. Admiral Jerrit should be able to find out what happened."

"Hopefully we can prove our innocence in this attack."

Another council member spoke up. "We also must consider that a faction with the Makeo has done this."

"Anything and everything is possible."

There was equal suspicion in the Makeo council chamber. Three of the members left in protest and the President had arguments with two others. The President on her part tried to convince the other members that the level of military cooperation was unprecedented and should prove their good faith.

"I find it unlikely that such a blatant attack would not be followed up by a massive attack."

"Madam President, once the public finds out about this; and they will find out sooner than later, they'll wonder why we haven't reacted stronger?"

"We'll just have to deal with that problem when it arises."

"And don't forget that General Hecor has tremendous support from the military and the public. He may not be so patient."

"Yes, some have said he's more popular than we are."

The President stared serenely. "But even General Hecor would have to admit that the Benari's gesture of open military access is unprecedented. I think we can count on General Hecor to follow orders. He's a good soldier."

* *

Although the Makeo and the Benari had governmental control

over sixty per cent of the galaxy, there were vast territories that were under loose consortiums or some without any control. These were often dangerous realms; places that frequently had power struggles and vicious battles. It wasn't uncommon to have sudden leadership changes through governmental coups.

The Mulor collective was a planetary system orbiting binary stars in a minimally inhabited quadrant. The warlike Bulori people were the dominant force and had been dealing with insurgencies for the past thirty years. On one of the desert planets the most successful insurgent movement, those of the Brutaha race had made significant advances under the leadership of the famous mercenary soldier, Talisa Caru.

Since the planet had some populated Brutaha cities, a full frontal assault on the occupying Bulori would have caused too many civilian casualties. The Brutaha had established a foothold in a mountainous region directly across from the strategic landscape confiscated by the Bulori. In the midst of a weapons exchange, Talisa Caru, a beautiful female with long wavy white hair, tanned face, turquoise eyes and a thin muscular body stood up from a high rock outcropping, holding onto a pair of binoculars.

A rocket whistled overhead, prompting her to duck behind the rock as it struck a nearby hill, blasting a wall of cloudy dust into the air. Three more missiles struck and impacted nearby peaks. Talisa shouted at her lead commander. "Hit the left flank! It's coming in from 50 degrees by 28."

Return fire from the Brutaha seem to quell the barrage. The commander ran up next to Talisa. "We can't hold this position for long. So far they haven't used orbital drops, but that's coming soon."

She stared upward at the twin suns. "I don't think so."

"They've done it before."

"Too close to their positions. They're only a mile away. Orbital drops are unreliable. We're too close for comfort."

"Can we really take that chance?"

"I think so. They have the upper hand. They don't need a

full assault. Why take the chance with orbital bombs when you can just advance slowly."

"We have to do something. Sooner or later we're going to have to retreat."

"We got to even the odds. They have us flanked on either side with their weapons. Eventually we'll have to concentrate on the flanks and we'll be vulnerable from a frontal assault."

"Awaiting your orders, Talisa?"

She thought for a moment. "We're going to make a partial withdrawal. Take some of our forces and protect the flanks. Our main force will be used to thwart a frontal assault. If we can hold until night, I'm going to take some troops in close to that mountain side. We might be able to knock out their command. Not the best plan, but it may be our only chance."

"I'll assemble our best fighters."

A fresh barrage of rockets struck around them, killing a few soldiers and injuring others. The Brutaha volleyed a few rockets back and this halted the Bulori barrage for a while. Soon missiles again dropped on the Brutaha positions, sending Talisa and the commander to the ground and filling their mouths with dirt and pebbles. They returned fire and then there was a silent respite. These small exchanges happened throughout the rest of the day until the afternoon sunlight diminished.

"Talisa, the flanks are holding."

She brushed her wavy hair out of her eyes. "They will until dark."

"I've assembled eight soldiers. I'll stay behind, because I know you're going to say that."

'That's adequate. You know if we're detected, they'll come at us the next day. You'll have to give the order to retreat."

"I understand."

She patted him on the arm. "You are a resilient people. You'll survive."

When night came it was so dark that one couldn't see much beyond their hand. In the absence of weapon's exchange, it was

41

eerie and quiet; lacking even the familiar animal noises. They couldn't remember when the blackness had been so suffocating; the perfect cover for their foray. The team donned their black camouflage clothes and masks, and checked their laser pistols and knives.

The commander approached Talisa. "We're getting some unusual energy spikes from the Bulori satellites."

"What do you mean?"

"I'm not sure. Power fluctuations."

"Keep an eye on it."

A satellite bomb was tracked by the commander, who ordered all the troops to take cover and prepare for impact. Instead of an explosion, the entire valley separating the combatants lit up in a phosphorous red blanket. Talisa leaped up and made a fist. "Damn, they got our playbook!"."

"Another incoming…"

"They'll be doing this all night."

"What are we going to do?"

Her head lowered. "They're adopting a siege strategy. They'll just sit back and wait us out. We have no choice but to retreat to a more advantageous position."

Bitter disappointment spread through the Brutaha forces as many just slumped over in defeat. They had fought valiantly but were overcome by a patient and well disciplined enemy. Talisa and the troops rested against the rocks in despair as the red glow settled over the valley.

Talisa instinctively drew her weapon when surprised by a three foot tall lizard like creature popping up from underground. The commander stopped her. "Don't shoot. It's a Monko."

"A what?"

"Monko. They live here. They're solitary beings. Harmless."

Stubby tailed with an orange belly, the Monko dusted off his greenish yellow skin. He spoke with a gravely voice. "Sorry if I startled you."

"What can we do for you?"

"It's what I can do for you."

The Commander nodded at Talisa. "Their species is neutral, but they don't like the idea of a Bulori take over."

"Very correct." insisted the Monko, wagging one of his three fingers. "A Brutaha defeat is not in our best interests."

"How can you help us?"

We live underground. Our world is a maze of tunnels and caves. I know a cave directly under the Bulori camp."

"You're willing to guide us?" she asked.

"Only you. Once you know the way, the others can follow."

The Commander pulled her aside. "Talisa, we should accompany you."

"These terms are acceptable. Besides, it's safer."

The Monko started down the hillside between rock buttresses which concealed a cave entrance. Once inside their flashlights scattered across the darkened walls. Breathing the stale air, Talisa could feel her boots slipping from the steep descent as the passageway became larger and opened up into a wider cavity.

The Monko would occasionally scamper ahead of her, only to stop and glimpse back at her. "We're at the lowest point."

She caught up to him. "How much further?"

"A little more."

"What's a little?"

The path became narrow at times and formidable boulders blocked their way. They climbed around and the cave walls narrowed until Talisa had to wedge her body through them. It opened once again to the largest cavern where there were plenty of stalagmites and stalactites; and apparently a dead end. Talisa was annoyed. "What's going on here? I don't see a way out."

The Monko pointed straight up. "We are directly below the Bulori camp."

"We have to climb?"

"No, that would be futile. There is no opening."

"Then why did you bring me here?"

"I said I would take you under the camp and I did. What more do you want?"

"Drilling equipment will give away our position."

The Monko hopped around giddily. "Your problem, not mine."

She stared contemptuously. "I'm going back."

He hustled in front of her and blinked rapidly. "Giving up so soon? What kind of warrior are you?"

"Excuse me?"

"Talisa Caru, you were never a defeatist?"

"Monko, do I know you?"

He pranced around her. "Know me? I should say so."

"I'm getting tired of this game." She crossed her arms. "So you say you know me. Where do you know me from?"

He stopped prancing, and gazed at her seriously. "I've known you for over two thousand years." His arms extended outward and he became the handsome villain she knew so well.

"Javensbee." She opened her palm to summon the Mist.

"Is there a problem?"

"I'm not sure."

"Talisa, you are more beautiful than ever. Eternity has not aged you one bit." He stepped around her delicately. "You are wondering why the Mist does not answer your summons."

"What did you do?"

"Nothing", he replied coyly. "But something has happened. Something the Mist has no power over. And as I previously told your comrade Dr. Tralin, I can't wait for you to find out what it is."

"What do you want from me?"

He gazed around the cavern. "Here you are on this puny piece of dust you call a planet, trying to save a people that will probably be conquered anyway; trying to save them. That's what I admire about you. You are invincible, and yet you are always trying to help the less fortunate."

"You wouldn't know about that, Javensbee. You spend your existence harming people. Lording over them."

"I don't disagree with you, but we both have something very much in common. Something that binds us together. Immortality. We can't die. And that has become so tiresome over the centuries. I want a change in my life. Yes, I could assume the role of sovereign ruler of this galaxy. But it seems so empty; so lonely. Yes, my love. What is supremacy without love?"

"You're not getting sentimental on me, Javensbee?"

He snickered, almost child like. "Perhaps I have become a romantic. And that is why I'm here with you. I have experienced many emotions; some good, and some bad. But I have yet to experience love. It is an emotion that I hope will alleviate the emptiness, the loneliness. It is what I need."

"Let me get this straight. You've come here after two hundred years to tell me that you love me? Because I can tell you right now I'd rather have the Monko."

"Make no mistake, Talisa. How I rule this galaxy is up to you."

"I'm to be your conscious? You've killed so many. Done such horrible things. And now you just want me to forget all that?"

Javensbee stroked her forearm. "I don't expect that. I understand our history. But you must understand that I am a product of my nature. And nature can be violent, uncaring and indiscriminate. It has to be controlled, right? And that is why I want you to help me."

"For the moment you have me at a disadvantage."

He pleaded with her. "Don't you see that we are much alike? Only you are good and I need to understand why good is preferable. We are going to live forever. You can not have love yourself. You will always outlive your mate. And I have yet to experience love. We are the perfect match."

"This is ridiculous. Absurd."

"Perhaps. But I'm going to make the first gesture. You really care about the Brutaha, so I am going to show you some good will. I will destroy your enemy. I will eliminate the entire race from existence."

"No, no, please don't do that? If you have any chance with me, that's not the way to win me over."

He smiled sardonically. "Fair enough. As I told you before, we are directly under the Bulori camp. Take my hand and we will confront the enemy."

"You'll practice restraint?"

He squeezed her hand and raised his other arm towards the cave roof, which melted into a five foot diameter hole. He yanked her off the ground and they flew up through the opening and out onto the Bulori ridge encampment. Shocked and surprised, Bulori officers drew their pistols and aimed at them.

The Bulori commander waved his pistol at Talisa. "Where did you come from?"

She held out her hands. "Don't shoot and you won't die."

He began to laugh, and then the others joined in. "There are just two of you and I am going to die?"

Javensbee stood with praying hands. "In the name of the Brutaha, please surrender?"

The commander laughed even louder. "Oh, you're priceless."

Talisa whispered to him. "Not exactly what I'd have said."

"I'm new at this."

"Do me one favor, don't kill everybody. This Bulori has no idea of who you are."

"I don't how you two got here. How we missed any drilling. But go back to your camp and offer terms of surrender and we'll let you live."

Javensbee whispered. "We have to put up with this?"

The commander nodded to his officers and they fired directly at them. The laser beams deflected easily off their chests and the commander ordered them to stop firing. "They got some kind of shielding!"

Talisa turned to the commander. "Now you've done it."

Javensbee pointed at a distant mountain peak and released a white hot beam of light that melted away the top five hundred feet into a mist of fire. When it was over the surface of the peak was sheered off and still steaming. The Bulori officers fell to the ground and covered their faces. The commander couldn't even swallow as Javensbee approached him.

"Who is the second in command?"

An officer timidly arose. "I am."

Javensbee thrust his arm towards the commander and a powerful wind blew him off the cliff, sending him screaming to his death. "So it appears we have a new commander now. I demand your entire army to withdraw from this planet immediately."

Talisa tugged on his vest. "They do have rights to the southern territory."

"All right, withdraw to the southern territories."

"It will be difficult to explain to my leaders."

"You'll have to convince them that I will eliminate any that don't comply."

He shouted to the rest of them. "Okay everybody. You heard him. Let's get out of here fast."

Talisa shrugged her shoulders. "Dramatic, if not overdone. But your mercy surprised me.'

"Then there is hope for us?"

"I don't know about that at the moment. Unless you want to tell me why I am unable to summon the Mist?"

"You will just have to find that out yourself. And believe me; I really can't wait for that to happen. But for now I must resume my main objective. I am not as yet convinced that you see things my way. Certainly not a future relationship with your sworn enemy. So for now, I bid you farewell." He changed back into the Monko, winked slowly with one of his big eyes and then vanished.

THREE

THE BENARI AND MAKEO HIGH councils met in the round chambers at the Makeo home world system. The President and the Chancellor sat across from each other, joined by their perspective aides. It was a delicate arbitration, one that would determine the future of galactic relations. It was cordial, yet there was distrust on both sides. The Makeo President spoke with great passion. "Chancellor, you must understand that I have a restive populace. Many, including those of our military establishment, believe the Benari was involved in these acts of aggression."

"I can understand, but we have been more than accommodating with our military operational transparency."

"We have received unprecedented access and that is primarily why we have trust between our governments at this juncture. But even I have some suspicion there may be a silent force within your military even unknown to yourselves."

"Even if that were true, we would be the first to expose such a faction. To what end would it advance our cause to have a military confrontation with your empire?"

"I agree. And that is why my government is giving you the

benefit of the doubt. But I must warn you that my government will grow impatient if we sense there is any cover up or deception."

Slightly irritated, the Chancellor swiveled in his chair. "Madam President, what would you have us do? We've been extremely cooperative."

"I'm concerned that we do not have safeguards in place for an impending emergency. What if a hair trigger response would lead to war?"

A Benarian diplomat spoke up. "Excuse me, but I may have a possible compromise. We form a joint task force, equal partners, to investigate any future incidents."

A Makeo diplomat responded strongly. "Out of the question! A joint force? We're the ones who were attacked."

The Makeo President held up her hand. "That is not an unreasonable solution. I would have to negotiate with our military, but I don't see much resistance coming from them if it leads to cooperative information."

Another Benarian interrupted. "I should say not. We've already given you too much of our military secrets already."

"He's right", the chancellor remarked. "I've had problems within my own ranks. Many have questioned my decisions."

"Then we're back to the beginning. These negotiations may be more difficult than I thought. We are certainly the children of warriors past."

The Makeo President seemed resigned. "Don't we owe it to our children to avoid the mistakes of our ancestors?"

"Eloquent words. But is that enough?"

The Chancellor silenced everyone with a knock on the counter. "I think we all agree in this room that war is to be avoided at all costs. The problem is mistrust. We must overcome that mistrust.

The President nodded. "On that we agree. Our militaries may have different opinions, but we are democratic societies and we must put our differences aside. Fighting among ourselves is a disservice to our people. Debate is acceptable. Rage is not."

* *

Dr. Tralin rested against his cliff top balcony rail at mid day and studied a reflective object in the distant sky. Now visible as a sleek dagger like spacecraft, it maneuvered over the valley and dipped towards an extended platform directly below him. The nosecone flared upwards and it landed gently on the port. Tralin went inside and stood near an elevator that delivered Talisa Caru up to him.

"Good to see you, Tralin. Even under these circumstances."

He chuckled. "It's always amusing to refer to our current names. Keeps thing orderly."

"I never thought we'd be here in this situation."

"It is perplexing. I have no explanation. And to the fact that Javensbee is seeking a lover, that really surprises me."

"You think you're surprised? I'm just plain disturbed."

"Javensbee has never had guidance. In many ways he's a child."

"Then he should be looking for a mother, not a lover."

"One fact is indisputable. He has the power to destroy an entire quadrant of the galaxy and yet has chosen not to."

"And you have no idea why the Mist is helpless?"

"I'm no closer to that answer since Javensbee first appeared. I do know that Golbot is somewhere in the Yireian Nebula on some kind of treasure hunt."

"He's been chasing the Btelis elixir pools for the past five hundred years. You'd think he'd figure out by now that it's a myth."

"Golbot will tell you that myth is always based in fact. And he does have all the time he needs to search."

"What about Ceylar?"

"I contacted his colleague, Dr. Wison. She hasn't seen in over three years."

"Then it may be Ceylar that's the key to this mystery." She placed both hands on her hips. "So where do we go from here?

The thought of being Javensbee's lover is not an appetizing option."

"You have a fast ship. Let's find Golbot."

"You haven't been on a deep space flight for many years?"

He reluctantly nodded. "And I'm not looking forward to it. There's a certain comfort about staying in one place. And to think, I was just contemplating what new identity I was going to assume after being the venerable Dr. Tralin."

"I'll try to make the trip as uneventful as possible."

* *

Dengy rested his head against his bed pillow as his wife just returned from the bathroom. He was relaxed and content, thinking about the previous day at the lab. Dressed in a night shirt, Ale jumped onto the bed and nuzzled up to him. "You seem lost in thought?"

"I'm just thinking about what a wonderful wife and companion I have. And how lucky I am to have her."

She furled her brow. "Is that right? Because I was just thinking the same thing; how lucky you are to have me."

He playfully hit her with the pillow. "Okay, I was really thinking about today's tests. That retroviral dislocation had positive results."

She seemed upset. "There goes my husband. I think I married a robot. Work has you consumed night and day."

"I know I can get a little intense. It's just that good results mark progress. You can't blame me for getting excited about that."

"I guess not. But we're far from real progress, Dengy."

A sweet smelling air freshener wafted into the room. Dengy pulled her closer to him and kissed her. Just as the mood became romantic, he brought up work again. "We did have a reading indicating a spike."

She stretched out flat on her back and stared at the ceiling.

"You're impossible. You have to let go when we're home. You know, have a life."

"You're right, I'm being selfish."

"Dengy, why don't we take the day off tomorrow? Do something fun."

"What if tomorrow brings a breakthrough?"

"You're so obsessed. Nothing I've said is getting through. You're a brilliant scientist and your time will come. But you should relax once in a while."

Dengy noticed a blinking red light on his bedroom wall monitor screen. 'This may be an important message."

"Ignore it. We'll get in the morning."

He activated the screen and a government official appeared with the official seals of the Benari and Makeo. "This is a special joint declaration. I now turn it over to the Benarian Chancellor."

The Makeo President sat next to him as he began to speak. "Citizens of the galaxy, as you may be aware there have been several attacks on Makeo property, as well as Benari property that have grave implications for both governments. There has also been evidence that a faction using Benari style vessels has been identified in one of the attacks. Let me assure all citizens that in no way the Benari government is responsible for these attacks. While investigations are ongoing, it is hopeful that full cooperation between our governments will build trust and that together we will find discover the perpetrators"

"I fully concur with the Chancellor. These have been difficult times for both our governments. We do not believe these attacks have come from our Benari friends. But this does not belie the fact that many of our Makeo citizens have been killed. And this we can not accept without having an answer. I must emphasize there are members of both governments that do not wish to take a conciliatory stance on these matters. But this is a time for diplomacy and cooperation. War must be averted under any circumstance. I now turn it back to the Chancellor."

"Thank you, Madam President. We have had lasting peace for over ninety years and in those early days our governments seemed to have a much closer working relationship militarily and economically. Over the years we have become less interactive. This is going to change. For this reason we are going to form a neutral joint council. I'll allow the President to explain."

"Each side will send ten delegates with staff and will report directly to our high councils. This new council will have immediate decision making in case of an emergency. It is important that they can react before even consulting our high councils. Any long term military venture would have to be approved by our governments. Until further notice, on behalf of the Benarian Chancellor and myself, peace and security to both our nations."

* *

Talisa and Dr. Tralin comfortably cruised at tremendous speeds towards the Yireian Nebula. Her space craft was luxuriously equipped with couches lining both sides of the cabin between the cockpit and sleeping quarters. While motion was undetectable, starlight streaked outside the rectangular windows. Talisa wandered up to the cockpit, where Dr. Tralin sat in the co-pilot's chair. "You seem distracted?"

He blinked, and then focused on her. "The long years between Javensbee were often tedious. But at least we knew we had Javensbee under control."

"How do you think I feel? I'm the object of his affection."

"If that is truly his intention."

She stretched out both arms across the top of the console. "I have to be honest, the last five hundred years have begun to grate on me. I never thought that I would become fatigued by eternity."

"Time has that effect."

"Tell me, Tralin. What identity were you going to assume next?"

He chuckled. "I did give it a little thought. Hide out a few years, reinventing myself as some kind of merchant. Not exciting, but obscurity. After a turn as the venerable Dr. Tralin, I need an inconspicuous occupation."

"Thinking back, my best role was as an intergalactic passenger ferry pilot. Did several routes in the Muraiunipotalio sector. Not much action, never was attacked by a menacing force. Can you imagine my best times were simply shuttling passengers back and forth?"

"I understand that. One of my best roles was a pharmacist on a small planet where they'd just sent their first rocket into space. It was an uneventful life. But I met some of the most wonderful, kind people. I miss them."

"Ever go back to them?"

"No. It would have been self indulgent. It was their world, their moment."

She adjusted a few controls. "Not that I haven't had exciting jobs. Had a lot of assassination attempts. Gave up counting. I had more fun just trying to figure out where the next one was coming from."

"I was a diplomat a few times. Once I had a difficult dilemma. I had to negotiate a peace treaty with a former world I had lived on."

"How did you manage that?"

"I gave all the glory to my subordinate and was accidentally killed in a shuttle mishap. Everything worked out fine."

"It's amazing all the things we've done. But none of that can prepare me for the role of the Songster's bride."

"Let's hope Golbot has some answers."

The Yireian Nebula was still a great distance away. Although it was generally a hostile environment, the solar systems on the outskirts had planets that were sometimes visitor friendly, but not well policed. Tralin was uncertain of Golbot's whereabouts, but knew of a few rumored planets that were home to the elixir pools. They set a course for once such place; an elliptical world that was cold and dark and dusty as any. Sparsely populated, only the heartiest adventurers would lay claim to its surface.

In the hilly, rocky southern polar region, a village was propped up against a series of canyon entrances. It had a few paltry wood and stone huts and flat areas to land a spacecraft. On this particular night, the wind was especially brutal, whipping up granules of dirt against the face of a shroud covered blimp of a man waddling towards the front door of the only saloon. The ground was frozen and the wooden porch steps creaked under his weight. He flung open the door, sending a chilled sandy breeze across the splintery floor.

There were about ten patrons in the saloon, including a tall surly bartender, who just followed the stranger with probing eyes. "You Golbot of Herenia?"

"I got a dry throat. What's your best?"

"One hundred year old Verla. But it will cost you."

He pulled out several shiny coins. "I'll take the whole bottle."

The bartender cupped the coins and drew them to him. "That's a year's salary."

"So I was expecting to talk to some people?"

The bartender pointed over to a table with one humanoid and two other creatures with eyes in their torsos and arms protruding out of their necks. Golbot opened the bottle cork with his teeth, gulped a mouthful and then walked over to the table. The humanoid licked his lips. "So you're the famous treasure hunter?"

One of the little ones whispered to the other in a female voice. "Doesn't look like very much."

"Listen sonny, I didn't come here to socialize. Who's the guide?"

"I'm Billings, your guide. I presume you have our payment?"

"Half now, half upon completion."

Billings counted the valuable mineral bars. "Looks right. These two are with me and two others will join us tomorrow."

"You're certain the elixir is here?"

"We wouldn't be here if it weren't. I know my business. But be aware, there are a lot of competitors that would kill for my information. That's why we're hoofing it tomorrow. Won't be using vessels."

"I'm curious. If you know where the elixir is, why don't you just get it for yourselves?"

"Golbot, you are obviously a man willing to handle such a rare and desired commodity. The elixir is sacred to some, money to others. I'm interested in saving my own neck. I'm happy with your payment. You can have the fame and what it brings."

He poured everybody a drink. "Then we have a deal."

"We'll leave early tomorrow."

The morning weather wasn't any better than the previous night. A strong wind blew across the village, stirring up a greenish brown dust that obscured much of the sunlight. Billings, his two torso friends and two other humanoids awaited Golbot, who was just emerging from his ship. He trudged over to the search party with garments flung around his forehead and chin. They all carried leather bags full of tools, flashlights, nutritional packets and locater devices.

"Ready to go?"

Golbot wiped off a saliva drop. "How far?"

"Through them rocks, about six hours if we make good time."

"Lead on."

The guide waved and they followed in single file. The canyon opening was hidden from the saloon; visible only when they hiked through a path of boulders. The canyon path was at least twenty feet wide with cliffs mostly obscured by the thickening dusty atmosphere. Their boots crunched the sharp gravely trail where the minimal sunlight barely revealed a smattering of shrubs and weeds.

After two hours in the canyon, Billings held up his hand and they stopped.

"What's up?"

He pointed to the entrance of a smaller canyon. 'We got to go through there. It'll be tighter and we'll be vulnerable to attack."

"Robbers?"

"No, this is Praxon territory."

"What the hell's a Praxon?"

Billings smiled wearily. "A nasty critter. They won't attack us out here, but the smaller canyons are ideal to pounce."

"I haven't seen any wildlife out here."

"Oh, there's plenty out here. They just know better to keep out of sight."

They pressed on cautiously into the offshoot canyon that had several twists and blind corners. The wind picked up through the narrower path and the greenish brown dust smacked their faces. After a while one of the search party members lagged behind. Without warning, a large reptilian creature leaped off the side of a rock and plunged its dagger like teeth into the top of the man's head. Blood squirted everywhere as the creature grabbed his shoulders and carried him off hastily into the recesses of the craggy cliff. The rest of he party fired lasers, but the creature had vanished.

"Praxon!"

They formed a circle and waited for the next attack. A few minutes passed by in silence. Golbot lowered his pistol. "I think they're gone."

Billings dropped his hand. "Think so? I've dealt with Praxon. They don't like to directly challenge you. But you can bet their watching us."

One man spoke up. "I think we should go back."

Billings laughed. "Okay. Good luck."

The man thought wisely. "No, I think I'll stay."

Golbot cleared his throat. "Let me go ahead."

"Are you crazy?"

"I've dealt with more ornery beasts than these."

"They'll tear you apart. But if you insist, it's your funeral. I'm happy with the partial payment."

Golbot tucked his pistol away in his garments and started walking towards the next blind bend. He studied the sides of the rocks carefully for any sign of movement. Except for the wind, nothing seemed unusual. And then he heard a rustling above, the first indication he was being stalked. He ambled confidently through the canyon, gazing upward as the noises increased all around him. Ahead of him a Praxon blocked the path as glimpses of other shadowy figures darted across the ridges. A Praxon jumped directly on top of him and tried biting into his scalp. He grabbed the creature's neck and with one powerful yank tossed it to the ground. Another Praxon joined the attack and soon others ripped into his garments and tried tearing his limbs apart. Faced with chomping mouths full of dripping saliva and razor sharp teeth, Golbot was eventually wrestled to the ground and smothered by hydra like head snaps and vicious scraping claws. Weathering the attack with impunity, Golbot managed to remove his pistol and shot a few laser blasts directly into their stomachs. Two of them died instantly, while the others scattered as he purposely missed harming them. Garments torn and flesh exposed, he draped the remaining cloth around his chest and stomach.

Billings and the others ran around the corner, stunned to find Golbot still alive. "Where's the Praxon?"

"They had enough. They ran."

"You got to be kidding me. You survived?"

"Guess I got lucky."

"So, should we go on?"

"How much further?"

"About another hour through this and then it opens up into a larger gorge."

Golbot nodded. "I don't think they'll attack us again."

"These things don't frighten easily."

He grabbed billings coat. "You aren't fooling with me? The elixir's here, right?"

"Yeah, yeah, of course."

Still bathed in dust, they proceeded through the narrow canyon until it opened up to a much wider passage. Billings stopped and pointed over at a cave entrance about ten feet up into the cliff. "The elixir is in there."

Golbot surveyed the immediate area. "Are you sure? Isn't it supposed to be guarded by some kind of priests?"

"Those are just stories. It's right in there. Be my guest."

Golbot ventured ahead towards the cave and the rest followed. He ducked inside and flashed his light across the walls. Billings removed a lantern from his pack and illuminated the entire cave; which was more of a shallow cavern. Against the wall was a wooden table with an old plastic jug placed on it. Golbot knew he'd been set up and tipped the table over and spilled water out of the jug. He turned and found them with pistols drawn. "So it was all a hoax?"

"We appreciate the payment. And nobody's going to find you here."

Billings aimed at Golbot's head and fired the laser beam at his face. To his shock, the beam just deflected off his face. Golbot ran at Billings, picked him up off the ground and threw him head first into the cave wall, crushing his skull. He then grabbed the torso beings by their arms and swung them around like helicopters, releasing them into the wall, killing them instantly. The one man left ran away, where he would eventually become lunch for the Praxon.

Disappointed, Golbot used a device to summon his ship; which appeared overhead. He beamed up and returned to the village; not in the best of moods. He smashed his stubby fists through the saloon door and the bartender's expression turned to horror. Golbot ran towards him and he fell backwards against a row of bottles, breaking several of them. Golbot charged through the guard rail, splintering the wood and then wrapping his fingers around his throat. "You set me up!"

"No! It wasn't me! I swear."

"Yeah, right. How much did they pay you?"

"Nothing, I swear."

"I think I'll pull one arm off now, the other in a few minutes." Other patrons considered helping the bartender, but a swift gaze from Golbot changed their minds.

"I'll pay you back. Just don't kill me."

Golbot's fingers relaxed around his throat. "You'll pay even more."

"Anything you want." He peeked up over Golbot,s shoulder. "There's some people back there that want to talk to you."

Golbot turned around, but did not immediately recognize them. He walked towards them and began to laugh. "Well, well, if it isn't the Mist. Out here in the middle of nowhere."

"Sit down, Golbot."

"Tralin, I didn't think you got out much. Hello, Talisa."

"I still see you're up to your old tricks. Wrecking a bar."

He sat down at the table. "Just a business disagreement."

"Another false lead?"

"So why are you two here?"

"Javensbee's back."

He grinned. "Then let's just dispel with the little asshole."

"It's not that easy. We can't summon the Mist. That's why we had to track you down. And now that we find everything's right with you, we know that something's happened to Ceylar."

"Where is he?"

"No idea. He's gone missing."

"You think Javensbee's done something to him?"

Tralin played with is goatee. "I don't think so. He claims he had nothing to do with it."

"Then the galaxy is at his mercy."

"He's starting a war between the Benari and Makeo."

"There's more", Talisa quipped. "He's in love with me. I think he wants to make me his queen."

Golbot laughed so hard his veins popped. "He'd be a good provider, that's for sure. So how are we going to stop him?"

"We have to find Ceylar. We have some ideas of where to start."

Golbot stood up. "Then I suggest Talisa prepares her fancy ship ready for departure. I've got one more thing I've got to do."

"Be quick."

To the bartender's dismay, Golbot reached his arms around one of the support pillars and began to shake it violently. As patrons ran out of the saloon, the pillar collapsed and part of the ceiling emptied onto the tables. Unfazed, Golbot shot his pistol indiscriminately at the walls and other supports, causing the entire ceiling and walls to crumble to the ground. Amidst the rubble and dust of the flattened building, he aimed one of his fat fingers at the bartender. "I don't like being set up."

Talisa waited for Golbot by the door of her vessel. "I suppose I have to tow your piece of shit garbage scow?"

"Yeah."

Comfortable within the confines of her ship, Golbot had just taken his first molecular shower in months. Reunited after so many years, they reminisced on cabin couches. "I'm not used to such luxury. But I got to say, this isn't bad for a girl's ship."

"It pleases me you approve."

"So we have no idea where Ceylar is?"

"We're on our way to meet a colleague of his."

"Have you warned the Benari and Makeo about Javensbee?"

Tralin's face withered in frustration. "Tell them what? The Mist can't stop Javensbee. Even if they believed us, it wouldn't stop him. It might even push him to more devastation. Right now the only thing holding him back is his professed love for Talisa."

"Lucky me. But I agree with Tralin. We need to find Ceylar. For some reason he is unwilling, or unable to bond with the Mist."

FOUR

THE PLANET OF KATUS WAS one of the gems of the Makeo Empire. Far from its home star, it was mostly covered in thick ice over deep frigid oceans. The only city, a uniquely self contained paradise of well manicured gardens and showcase front lawns, was housed in a phosphorescent red oblong building near a rocky outcrop of land. The population of 22,000 miners and their families often bragged that one could eat off their pristine streets. On this planet alone, they produced the most valuable mineral for energy use known. Katus was so important that a military base was in orbit solely for the protection of its operation.

Although mining transport vessels were regularly scheduled on a daily basis, twice weekly Katus awaited the arrival of bulky cargo ships at the internal docking platforms. On one such uneventful day a Benarian cargo ship was cleared by the military base to land. It slowly descended through the thin atmosphere and swayed gently through the sturdy docking doors, which opened and closed behind it. The indigenous crew hustled towards the ship to unload its cargo.

The first sign of a problem came when the foreman was unable to communicate with the cargo personnel. After several unsuccessful attempts the foreman was about to contact his superior when the doors opened up and a blitz of three foot long gray and black insects instantly covered the floors and walls. The docking crew was consumed at such rapidity that no one was able to sound any alarms. The insects entered opened doors and vents, voraciously attacking anyone they came upon. Once they finished in one section, they moved onto others, crawling over thousands of citizens and devouring the flesh cleanly off their skeletons. Mothers tried to shield children, but were all torn to shreds by their powerful jaws. Screams were heard everywhere, and before any citizen could contact the military base, they were eaten alive.

The insects rippled over the floors, ceilings, atriums, patios, offices and eventually the mines below in blurring waves, killing all those they encountered. Some workers did try to warn the miners, but were stripped of every piece of meat on their bones. Within fifteen minutes of the original attack, more than fifty per cent of the population had been decimated.

The Songster streaked as a flash of light towards the orbiting military base, where nobody had an indication of the carnage below. Javensbee assumed his humanoid form; and extended both arms and legs out and splattered against the outer hull of the station. He melted through the metal surface and into the main control room where several Makeo crew were sucked out into space. An automated force field returned integrity to the control room and the environment was immediately restored.

The military base personnel were still unaware of the events on the planet or that Javensbee now moved freely throughout their circuitry. In a sudden overload of all systems, the main control room force field was destabilized and the environmental controls failed. Fortunately the room had been evacuated the remainder of the crew were able to slip into survival suits. Javensbee abandoned the station and flew off into deep space. A few hours later they were able to restore most of the systems and tried to communicate with the city below.

Unable to elicit a response, the first reconnaissance team landed a shuttle in the docking area. Dressed in full hazardous survival gear they plodded out of the shuttle and the lead officer addressed the station commander. "We're in. There's a Benarian cargo ship, some other vessels. No sign of life---oh, no! Skeletons everywhere! Everybody's picked to the bone. I'm going to take an analysis." He waved a recording device over one of them. "There seems to be some traces of alien DNA. I'm getting a reading now. It appears to be of insect origin. Spinorta Baliocisis Teperol."

The team moved into the adjacent room and found more of the dead. It wasn't until the third room they found the first dead Spinorta carcass. "These things are huge! I'd say over three feet in length. They're all expired. The readings show they starved to death. We've got some evidence of cannibalism, too."

A further search revealed the first survivors who had managed to seal themselves off. They were terrified and had several injuries, including some with chunks of flesh hanging off their arms and shoulders. Soon it became apparent that only nine hundred and fifty of a population of 22,000 had survived. An order was immediately given to evacuate everyone off the planet.

Two days later the inhabitants of the galaxy would learn about the massacre at Katus. The newly appointed joint council prepared to address the full assembly of Benarian and Makeo government officials at the Makeo home world. The lead investigator stood in the center of the circular chamber and spoke in dire tones. "This briefing is the culmination of the investigation of the events that transpired on Katus. It is by official designation council order 3569.051. We have concluded that the city had been the subject of a deliberate biological attack with genetically altered Spinorta Baliocisis Teperol. As many of you know that Spinorta are indigenous to tropical eco systems and are normally one to two inches in length. They are a ground burrowing insect, but do occasionally swarm. During this cycle the Spinorta have enhanced appetites. These Spinorta were genetically altered and their size dictated their appetites. It is also the conclusion of our scientists that this insect was the ideal life form to accomplish genocide on this scale. Due to this genetic reconfiguration, their metabolism was such that these Spinorta could only survive a few hours at best. Thus the city was riddled with Spinorta corpses."

"How did they get there?"

"They were transported in a Benarian cargo ship that contained Spinorta stasis chambers. They were thawed and released. The transport was fully automated; no crew." He looked down at the floor. "There is one other disturbing fact. Upon full examination of the cargo vessel, we found official Benarian security codes."

The Makeo President stood. "Are you saying that the codes were compromised?"

"I'm saying that these codes enabled this vessel to dock will full clearance."

Genral Hecor leaped up from his chair behind the council. "Only the Benarian military have access to these codes!"

"General Hecor, know your place!"

He turned to the Makeo President. "With all due respect, Madam President. This is a breach of the utmost concern."

The Chancellor tried to calm everyone. "Madam President, the General is right to express outrage. But I assure you, there is no high level conspiracy here. This matter has grave implications. War would be catastrophic."

"If there is a spy, a secret network, how Chancellor are you going to uncover it?"

"Our military in concert with yours should be able to discover the saboteurs."

Hecor protested. "Your military could be in on it."

The President turned to him, annoyed. "That will be enough. You are addressing an elected official of the Benarian Empire. You must give him respect. One more outburst and I will have you removed."

Hecor backed away sheepishly. "I apologize. My apologies to the Benarian Chancellor."

"I accept the General's apology. And I believe we all need to lower the tension in this room. Trust has been eroded, and trust must be restored. Perhaps we should suspend lower level contacts between our societies and allow the special joint council to continue its investigation."

The Makeo President concurred. "Yes, we have an intolerable situation and we must find a way out. I will do everything possible to avoid war. The Makeo do not want war."

"Then we are in agreement."

The meeting was called to an end and General Hecor retreated hastily down the corridor with the President. He was very upset, swinging his arms everywhere. "Mam, this is not the time to be timid."

"I understand your feelings on this matter. But if you're asking me to abandon peace for suspicion, I will not."

"I warn you, Madam President, the Katus massacre could bring your government down if we do not act."

* *

Dr. Tralin removed some articles from his desk at his Cliffside estate. He secured and saved all his computer programs and files, and then packed a minimal amount of clothes into his suitcase. He was alerted by an incoming shuttle that had landed on the front lawn near the main entry door. Puzzled by the sudden invitation, Dengy exited the shuttle was admitted into the house. "You wanted to see me, Dr. Tralin?"

"Yes, yes, please come in and sit down."

Dengy noticed the suitcase. "Are you going somewhere?"

Tralin poured himself a drink. "Thirsty?"

"No, sir."

"I'm taking an extended leave from the institution. I wanted to tell you personally."

"Are you ill?"

"I'm in good health. There's going to be a new director

here. He will be assigned from the military. The Katus event has changed everything."

"Do you think war's inevitable?"

"Dengy, everything is unknown at this time. However, it is quite probable that your experiments will be canceled. I have suggested to the new director that your work should continue, but I have little input at this moment. But remember, I believe your work is very promising. Never give up on it."

"I'm disappointed you're leaving us. And not just because of me."

"Hopefully we'll meet again and I can assume my role at the institution. And say goodbye to that lovely wife of yours."

Dengy nodded once, and then headed towards the front door; almost bumping into Talisa Caru. Golbot followed closely and sneered at him. Dengy glanced back one last time, and then left the house.

Golbot slapped Tralin on the back. "See you're ready?"

He frowned. "There's nothing left for me here."

"It's always a mixed feeling when one has to forsake an identity."

"Let's not get weepy", Golbot joked. "We've got a lot of work ahead of us."

"Yes, I've notified Dr. Wison. She's expecting us."

* *

General Hecor, Lieutenant Fecan and four of his most trusted personal guard traveled unescorted through the blackness of space. Each one of their stretched faces displayed desperate resolve as they flew by red giants, white dwarfs, colorful nebulas and vibrant neutron stars. They slowed to sub-light speed and settled into orbit around a desert planet near an orange star system.

Hecor ordered two of his guards to stay with the vessel while he and the others beamed down to the crowded, disorganized streets of a dirty town. There were beings from many worlds applying their trades; some with two heads, ten eyes, multiple limbs and gooey skin. Most of the bazaar booths were wooden and decrepit with merchants bartering their way to a meager existence. Food odors, some pleasant but mostly foul, wafted up into the sky while fruit the size of small children were displayed along the roadside.

Fecan led the way and the guards followed behind their general. A few merchants tried to stop them and show their wares, but were pushed aside. "You'd think our friend would keep better company?"

"Yes, General. I too am repulsed by this place."

"It just plain stinks."

Fecan held up his arm and halted the party. "I believe that merchant selling incense is our contact."

They walked over to the pudgy little creature, who tried to sell them a stick.

The General pushed in front of Fecan. "Not interested. But I am interested in a certain heat product?"

The merchant immediately closed up his booth. "Come this way."

They followed him through a few back streets and into an alley lined with wooden doors. The merchant knocked three times, twice, and then one hard knock. He stepped aside as the door opened up into a room with one table and a few chairs. "Anyone here? We have visitors."

A curtain swept aside and Javensbee, recognized as Oribud of Galcon, entered the room. "Ahh, General; here we are for our inevitable meeting."

He laughed. "Judging by this place, you sure know how to live."

"So what brings you here?"

"You know why I'm here. The weapon."

Javensbee delayed his response. "Oh, you want the weapon?"

"Don't play games, Oribud. Name your price."

"So, you think it's just a matter of price?"

"Come on, everybody's got their price."

"True, and one day I may name it." He paced around the room. "Katus was an awful thing. Your government must be ready to pay for the weapon?"

"What makes you think I'm here on behalf of my government?"

"General, I'm going to tell you something that I once told your Lieutenant. I don't deal with hired help."

Hecor became unleashed and ranted. "What! How dare you! I am the commanding General of the Makeo Empire."

"Exactly. Hired help."

"I could kill you where you stand."

Javensbee was dismissive to the point of exasperation. "General Hecor, you and I know that if you terminate me, all hopes of getting the weapon will be gone. Besides, once you hear my terms you will be quite satisfied."

Hecor's right eye closed. "All right. You win. You think I'm hired help, I'm going to prove differently."

* *

Tralin, Caru and Gobot approached a system with hundreds of planets where the eighteenth one nearest to the main star was their destination. After gaining permission to land at an expansive scientific complex, they docked the ship and disembarked. They found Dr. Wison, a tall translucent bald headed humanoid with tear drop eyes seated at her office desk surrounded by aquariums.

"Dr. Tralin, good to see you. It's been a long time."

"Thank you. And these are my colleagues."

"I am familiar with Talisa Caru's reputation. You, I'm not."

"Golbot of Herenia."

"I have made some discreet inquires since our last transmission."

Dr. Tralin curiously gazed at her. "Tell me, can I ask why Dr. Ceylar left you? You intimated some differences."

"He came to us three years ago. A preeminent biologist; an expert in botanical science. An authority on rare species."

"Always the authority", Golbot remarked sarcastically.

"He served here quite remarkably, but then I began to notice his behavior had changed. At first it was subtle; he became agitated over minor reasons. And then he began to lose his temper, often shouting."

"Did he ever discuss these issues with you?"

"We did speak about it, but he acted as if he didn't understand, or even acknowledge he was behaving this way. It all culminated when he almost destroyed a laboratory. We feared we might have to restrain him. After that, I had no choice but to relieve him of duty."

Golbot shook his head. "We're in trouble."

"He left soon after. It wasn't until you contacted me recently that I sent out a photograph and genetic code. I was surprised that the photograph had generated a first response. It turned out that he had gone to a planet named Jorafita and was involved with a series of legal difficulties. The best I can do for you is the name of the prison where Dr. Ceylar had been incarcerated."

"Thank You, Dr. Wison. That's something."

* *

The full council of the Makeo government met in the circular headquarters at the home world. The President and her staff were receiving an updated report on the Katus massacre. Strangely missing were any high military officers, whose absence had initially irritated the President. As the briefing intensified, no one noticed that the guards had slipped away. Unknown to all of them, a timer activated explosive was attached to the underside of the circular table.

Without anyone suspicious, the bomb blast expelled chunks

71

of sharp deadly metal in every direction and instantly murdered the council members. When rescue crews finally made it inside, there was carnage of unbelievable proportions. Word soon spread about the explosion and the next highest officer, The Minister of Health, prepared to succeed the President.

Almost panicked, the Minister of Health scurried around his office like a headless chicken. General Hecor barged in with a guard detail. "General, this is awful. I don't know what to do."

"Minister, you'll do nothing."

"What do you mean? I have to address our public."

"Place him under arrest."

"What? You can't do this to me!"

"Can't do what? Arrest a saboteur? Get him out of here."

As the guard led the Minister out of his office, Hecor made his way to the former President's office and sat down at the monitor to address the citizens of the galaxy. "A short time ago an explosive device killed the President and council in their chambers. We have definitive proof that the weapon was of Benarian origins. This confirms our suspicions that this attack, along with Katus and others are a deliberate attempt at destabilizing the relationships we have all accepted for the past ninety years. While we do not have evidence that the civilian government of the Benarian people is directly responsible, it is clear that some force within their military is at fault. As of now I am announcing that we are officially at war and I have assumed complete rule of the Makeo Empire. To those citizens of the Makeo, I assure you I have complete cooperation from our military. To the Benarian Chancellor I have issued orders to suspend all treaties and diplomatic relations. I will personally keep open communications with the Chancellor, but make no mistake that any hostile action will be met with an overwhelming response. As I speak, I have sent the sixth and seventh fleet to the Eminar quadrant where the Makeo will assume all control of what should have been our territory in the first place. I am giving all Benarian citizens 72 hours to evacuate Eminar space.

If any citizens remain, they will be arrested. I give this warning to the Benarian forces, if attacked we will respond. To all other non-Benarian citizens, you are welcome to stay."

Hecor ended the transmission.

The Benarian Chancellor sat in his office in a trance. Two of his Admirals flanked him. "I guess we have no option but to retaliate."

The Admirals stared somberly until one spoke. "Chancellor, that may not be the wisest strategy. The move to take over the Eminar quadrant is very clever of Hecor." He brought up a map on the monitor. "As you can see this territory is on the far side of the Makeo Empire; very distant from our nearest forces. The two Makeo fleets are more than enough to secure Eminar space. If we were to engage them, we would have to fight through their strongest forces."

"He's correct, Chancellor. That would leave our home world vulnerable. Hecor wants us to engage. It would be a mistake."

"Then what should we do?"

"I have some friends within the Makeo military. Let's see how much power Hecor really has. But for now, the best strategy is restraint"

"Very well. I'll give the order to surrender all Eminar bases and planets. I'll have to tell our citizens something, but I don't know what."

"Itt's wise to form some kind of future strategy. We have to assume Hecor will not stop at Eminar. We must anticipate his next move."

The two Makeo fleets, each comprised of twelve battle cruisers, two hundred smaller warships and six hundred support bombers and fighters, proceeded unchallenged to the Eminar quadrant. The Benarian military basses had already begun to evacuate, some ships passing the Makeo fleets as they fled. The civilian evacuation was not as efficient and led to some hysteria. Families were uncertain of what transports to take and the city streets were riddled with crying mothers and children. Some Benarians resisted and were arrested and brutalized by the Makeo police. Others quietly gathered what possessions they could carry and boarded any available vessels. There were angry Makeo citizens that attacked Benarians and the police refused to protect them.

The sixth fleet dispersed into the highly populated areas, taking up positions near and around most of the largest Benarian military bases. The seventh fleet would take positions in a much wider perimeter, patrolling the outer regions to repel a surprise attack. All twelve battle cruiser groups encircled the entire quadrant. Within twenty four hours, the Makeo military had completely sealed off Eminar.

Benarian citizens returned to their home world and related stories of Makeo brutality. Some claimed their houses were looted and burned, others showed physical scars. Mothers had broken arms trying to protect their children and others claimed they were raped. The Chancellor had hoped for some kind of apology, but none was given. That evening the Chancellor would address his woeful citizens.

* *

Talisa's ship darted across space towards the Jorafita home world. After hearing the Chancellor's speech, Golbot swore fervently. "I hate being at Javensbee's mercy! Playing his game's a losing one."

"At least his game is still playable."

"It still pisses me off."

A cockpit warning buzzer alerted Talisa. "We're slowing to sub-light."

Jorafita was a large planet with a varied eco system. Several metropolises were spread throughout high mountains, dry deserts and massive oceans. The prison complex was located in the hills near a lake. Talisa landed her ship near the front entrance that was guarded by androids and automated weaponry. They displayed their identification and were escorted to the warden's office.

"Come in, come in. Sit." The warden also sat down behind his desk. "When you sent me this picture of who you claimed to be Dr. Ceylar, we were quite mystified. We were unable to attain a bio scan of him."

"You seemed surprised his name was Ceylar?"

"We knew this man by the name of Andropodi."

Golbot eyed Talisa. "His real name."

"May we see him?"

"If he were here." Two guards entered the room and trained their weapons on them. "I apologize for this inconvenience. But this prisoner was a very dangerous criminal. Until we know who you really are, I'm going to have to detain you."

Tralin smiled. "The Benarian Chancellor will vouch for me."

The warden nodded to the guards, who left the room. "I'm certain we can clear this up. Again, I apologize for this awkward treatment."

Minute's later one guard returned and nodded to the warden. "Very good, Dr. Tralin. We had to be sure. This inmate Andropodi escaped and killed one of our guards. If you are his friends, hopefully you will help us find him."

"That's why we're here. We have no idea of where he is."

"Can you tell us why he was here?"

"Andropodi claimed he was a geologist. He was aiding a known syndicate transporting galgozite. We arrested him, held him for six months and then he escaped. No one has ever successfully escaped this prison. We still don't know how he did it. But he killed one guard and injured five others. We had film of the break and somehow a laser blast missed him. But that was the odd thing; the film shows what appears to be a direct hit."

"And you have no idea of his whereabouts?"

"He was in a cell with two others. One was released; the other still has some time to serve. I can arrange a meeting."

"That would be appreciated."

They were escorted through a labyrinth of jail cells until

75

they reached the humanoid prisoner. At first he objected to the visitors, but soon relented and stepped aside as they entered the cell.

Tralin held on to a vertical bar. "We'd like to ask you a few questions about one of your former cell mates. His name was Andropodi."

"What's he to you?"

"A friend. We're looking for him."

"I don't where he is."

Golbot removed an expensive mineral. "This is patosite. Memory coming back?"

The prisoner licked his lips. "Something's coming to mind."

"I thought so."

"I wasn't his only cell mate. He was much closer to this Dinklet."

"A what?"

Talisa smiled. "Toripodias Dinklartorlum."

"She's right. They're an insect race. They live on this planet not too far from here. This particular Dinklet was big drug dealer. They're all addicted to this stuff called tirithium. A controlled substance from a planet called Tiri."

"Do you know how we can find him?"

He eyed the patosite, which Golbot handed over to him. "These insects have weird names. Number names. He was 2N of 6 Billion."

The three of them left the cell as the prisoner kept flipping the bar in his hand. When he was alone, his eyes twinkled, the bar melted into his hand and he dematerialized into a shower of dust.

* *

Dengy and Ale sat quietly in he new director's office at the institute. He was nervous, she was circumspect; both expected the worst. The Director strolled in with a friendly expression.

"Thank you for being prompt. I realize my predecessor had great enthusiasm for your project."

"But you're canceling us?"

"Dengy, these are grave times. I do not have the luxury of continuing projects that do not benefit our national security. I will be suspending your experiments."

Ale lurched upward in her chair. "Hopefully only temporarily?"

Dengy closed his eyes. "It will never be revived. That's how these things work."

"I am sorry. My decision is final. I will be reassigning Ale to a new project. Her resume indicates some expertise in military applications?"

"That was a while ago."

"Perhaps. But that's where you're needed. They are developing a new sensor array."

"What about my husband?"

"The assignment is many light years from here. He will go with you, of course. But we have no assignments for him at this time."

"Maybe I should look at the bright side. It's a vacation."

Ale was miffed. "This is ridiculous. My husband has great talents."

"I'm sure he does."

Ale was about to continue her diatribe when he took her by the hand. "Come on, let's go. We're done here."

* *

The planet of Tiri was located in proximity of the Dinklet home world. It was close to its sun and had daytime temperatures exceeding 125 degrees. The tirithium plant thrived so well due to the wretched humidity. Heavily fortified, it was opportune that Talisa had once had a casual acquaintance with one of the top governors. She set her ship down in the baking sunlight where a protective shield enveloped the landing site. The governor welcomed them to his sprawling farm."

"Talisa Caru, it's been a long while. Good to see you."

"This is my friend Golbot of Herenia."

"Your message was something about needing tirithium?"

"I know it's a difficult request. But I need three kilograms."

His eyes popped out. "Even if you had the patosite, I could never part with that. I have exclusive contracts."

"I understand."

"Perhaps a gram will do?"

"No, that's not quite the amount we needed. We should be going."

"Can you stay for dinner?"

"No, I have a few other sellers to talk to."

"I don't think my competitors will sell either. But it's worth a try."

They went back to the ship and fled away a great distance from Tiri. "Golbot, did you get the codes?"

He removed a device from his pocket. "Just like you said."

Tralin grabbed the corner of a couch. "You were right about the governor."

"He would have parted with anything, but the tirithium. Now all we have to do is wait until dark."

Several hours later Talisa and Gobot dressed in black clothing and prepared for their excursion. "Thankfully we have the great Talisa Caru in this circumstance." Tralin seemed agitated with his uncharacteristic outburst.

She stared oddly. "Are you all right?"

Golbot studied a map. "We always leave him out of the thrill."

"Sorry, Tralin. Sop anyway, we have a small opening to beam in. We'll initiate a short pulse to avoid detection. Once inside, the security codes will adapt to us. We'll have to avoid the guards. Should be no problem."

"What happens if we detected?"

"If that happens before we get to the tirithium vaults, then we're out of luck. If we get that far, we'll have to confront the guards before we disable the codes. If one of them sounds the alarm, we'll be trapped. Tralin won't be able to rescue us."

"It appears I have some use after all."

Talisa flashed her beautiful smile. "You have the most important task. You beam us in, take the ship out of sensor range and then come back for us."

She maneuvered her vessel into a high orbit around Tiri and adapted a cloaked shield frequency. Armed with pistols and code busting devices, Tralin beamed them through a sliver of planetary shielding and immediately sped away from Tiri space. Even if the transport had of been detected by security, it would probably be dismissed as a common anomaly that occurs with most energy fields.

Talisa and Golbot hid inside a utility closet where they disabled the first security codes and crept towards the door at the far end of the corridor. When Golbot disarmed that door, they knew a guard would be posted on the other side. They opened the door, stunned the guard and remotely reprogrammed the camera to loop to the previous picture. They freely passed through another corridor that ended at a perpendicular intersection.

She whispered. "Get ready to jam the cameras. Two guards should be on either side at the far end."

They wearily stood at the crossway, disabled the camera codes, then swung around back to back and rendered both guards unconscious. They proceeded down the left side corridor and opened the door after disabling more cameras. "The main control room to the vault is on the other side. There could be four to five personnel in there. Once we knock them out, we can disable the vault codes."

"Let's do it."

They opened the door, the guards froze in place as Talisa stunned two of them near the control panel while the others fired lasers at Golbot's massive chest. Talisa rolled across the floor and stunned one more of them and Golbot stunned the last two. Talisa was free to disarm the vault codes from the security panel. "It's done. We're free to move on without further interference."

They passed through sliding door and into a wide hallway where a guard surprised them around the bend. Talisa dispatched him quickly and Golbot rested up against the final door at the end. "When this door opens, we're in the vault. Allow the guards to fire at us and that should distract them until we fire back."

The door opened and the guards aimed squarely into their chests. The beams dissipated and the guards were shot and fell to the floor unconscious. They hurriedly gathered the tirithium and signaled Tralin, who beamed them back to the ship as alarms rang throughout the facility.

Talisa ran up to the cockpit. "We've been detected."

"How could this happen?"

"I don't know, but I got a trick that always works."

Talisa slowed the ship jarringly to five hundred miles per hour, angled sharply behind an asteroid and dropped onto the surface. They hit the deck and jumped to their feet immediately as the pursuing ships passed them by.

"The governor will probably figure out it was you, Talisa."

"Yeah, but who cares? We got a date with a bug."

* *

General Hecor was in conference with Lieutenant Fecan, his security detail and five of his most trusted generals. Hecor had modified his personal headquarters to house the new seat of government. He surrounded himself with a circumference of monitor screens and sycophantic officers praising his greatness. "Has the Eminar evacuation been completed?"

"About ninety per cent, sir. Do you wish us to begin the incarceration of those that have not left?"

"No. We should be satisfied with compliance so far. We can afford some good will."

"All military bases have been commandeered by our forces."

"Excellent. I believe the seventh fleet can maintain order along the perimeter. Begin withdrawal of the sixth fleet and redeploy them along the Coremac system. But whatever you do, do not impinge on Coremac territory. That will keep the Benarians occupied with second guessing our motives."

"General, the Chancellor is waiting."

"Good. Greetings Chancellor. Before you begin with any accusations, we have decided to allow more time for your citizens to evacuate."

"I appreciate that, Hecor. Could I ask what other territories you wish to annex?"

"Cooperation like that led to the Katus massacre."

"Then perhaps you can tell me when we will resume some kind of diplomatic relations?"

"Chancellor, at this time I am only concerned about the Makeo. This transmission is over."

Lieutenant Fecan whispered to Hecor. "He's becoming impatient."

"I'll bet he is."

"What should I tell him?"

"Show him in."

Javensbee followed Fecan into the room. He stood in front of Hecor and his generals. "I was beginning to wonder if my presence was needed?"

"Oribud, we are no longer on that filthy dusty planet of yours. You are now at my headquarters, addressing the new Makeo leader."

He bowed his head graciously. "As it should be, General."

"So I am no longer the hired help."

"So it seems."

"What are terms, Oribud? And if you are elusive again, I will kill you where you stand."

"Not necessary, General. There will be no delay. My price for the weapon is not of a financial arrangement."

"After all this, you don't want payment?"

"My terms are extremely modest. I wish to be a member of your military. Specifically your ordinance officer. You can have as many missiles as you desire, but I will be the only one that can detonate them. I know that without insurance I am expendable."

"So the Galconian trader wants to serve me? You are correct about one thing. Killing you would defeat my purpose. You want to be my ordinance officer, the commission is yours. That's a reasonable price."

"Can I be so bold as to ask when my services will be required?"

"Let me ask you a question? What territory do you think is the most valuable in the galaxy?

"Commercially or militarily?"

"Both."

"That would be Relemark; situated between Benari and Makeo space."

Hecor leaned back in his chair, amused. "And if attacked, the Benari would have to defend it to the death?"

"I see your point."

"And one more thing, Oribud. Remember you are my ordinance officer, not my defense minister. In the future my plans are none of your business."

"Of course, forgive me."

* ** *

Dengy sat in a chair on the balcony of his new apartment and counted the vessels that traveled past his patio. He was bored, lonely and feeling as if he had no purpose in life as his wife assumed her new duties. His thoughts alternated from disgust to irrelevance and his prospects for some kind of assignment seemed remote. He just kept staring at the monotonous flow of vessels.

Ale came home and he barely rose to kiss her on the cheek. "I hate this as much as you do, Dengy."

"Why, you got a job."

She took two hard steps back. "Oh, it's my fault now?"

"No, I didn't mean it that way."

"Well I'm sorry that everything didn't work out the way you wanted it to. But that's just life. Everything doesn't have to revolve around you."

"What's that supposed to mean?"

"Come on, Dengy. You know what I mean. You sit here day after day and complain. Why don't you go out and find work. What's stopping you?"

"Oh, sure. My name's Dengy and I'm a brain scientist."

"You have many skills. You're just feeling sorry for yourself and you want to wallow here in your pity."

"Oh, that's real supportive."

"I'm sorry if I can't be sweeter. But I'm the one working. And for the life of me I can't figure out what I'm doing here."

"You got a job."

She flashed him an angry stare, turned around and stomped into her bedroom.

FIVE

CALMNESS DESCENDED UPON THE INHABITANTS of the galaxy after the
initial annexation of the Eminar Quadrant. Life in the territories
began to normalize as the Makeo indicated they would cooperate
with non-Benarian species. Once that General Hecor issued
decrees pursuing peaceful commerce, the Benarian Chancellor
had relayed some hopeful speeches to his own populace.

The Sixth fleet had positioned five battle cruisers and
hundreds of smaller attack vessels along the border of the
Coromac system; an important commercial region of Benarian
space. The Chancellor Complained vehemently about the Makeo
intimidation, but was unwilling to challenge them in battle. The
Coromac system statistically favored the Makeo.

The first news of direct encounters with the Makeo came
when their scout ships illegally searched Benarian supply vessels.
There were protests, but these tactics were at first only a matter of
inconvenience. When a large Benarian convoy was about to enter
Coromac space and was stopped by a Makeo battle cruiser, the
reality of direct conflict was eminently possible. The Chancellor
called for a meeting, but to his dismay General Hecor told

him that the Makeo would be controlling all trade throughout Coromac.

The Chancellor gathered his admirals in an emergency session. "We have a problem. What are we going to do?"

"No matter what you think of that little bastard, he is quite the tactician. Like Eminar, Coromac favors the Makeo. If we send a fleet, the Makeo can cut it off from behind. We'd have no way to respond. Unless you're prepared for all out war?"

Another admiral interrupted. "It would be militarily unwise to confront Hecor now."

The Chancellor turned pale. "We don't seem to have any good options."

"At least we have some in the Makeo military that are loyal to the previous treaty. I received some messages to that effect."

The chancellor resolutely sat upright in his chair. "All right. I want several contingencies on the table in the next five hours."

"We should still consider that Hecor desires an excuse for all out war."

"That very well may be. But time is running out. I've made my decision. I want a system we can annex."

* *

Talisa's ship slowed to sub-light upon entry into a solar system with seven planets and a treacherous asteroid belt. She dodged the rocks, occasionally shoving some aside on her way to the Dinklet planet. It was mostly a hot and dry desert with over twenty billion Dinklets spread out over thousands of cities. Although Dinklet architecture seemed primitive for a space fairing species, they had long mastered significant technological achievements.

Talisa gained permission to land in the capital city where she had an audience with a high official that had heard of her galactic prowess. They were escorted to a ceramic dome and waited for the official to arrive. Golbot kept complaining about the rancid smell of insect hygiene until Tralin silenced him when a heavily robed Dinklet with six hairy arms approached them.

He spoke in a hoarse, vibrating voice. "So you are the mercenary, Talisa Caru?"

"These are my friends, Dr. Tralin and Golbot."

"I've heard of the Dr. Tralin the great scientist. You sir, I do not know."

Golbot smirked. "Same here."

"We need to speak to one of your citizens. 2N of 6 billion."

"He is a prominent tirithium dealer. What is your business with him?"

"He may have some information about a friend."

"I can not guarantee he will see you. But I will give you information about where he conducts his deals."

"Thank you, sir. We appreciate your help."

They walked away. "This place still stinks."

Dinklets were flightless insects and traveled in shuttles that mimicked their anatomy. Talisa, Tralin and Golbot were in a shuttle that skipped across the lower elevations over rocky buttes and rippling sand dunes. They encircled a lone city in the middle of a barren plateau and landed near the main business center. Along with crawling Dinklets, several other species gathered around shops along the main causeway.

Golbot sniffed the air in disgust. "What now?"

"If this bug is as important as they say he is, we should get some answers." Talisa went over to one of the tirithium dealers. "I need some information?"

"You interested in my product?"

"No, I have something much better. The highest quality."

"Nonsense, my product is the highest quality."

"I think not. Do you know 2N of 6 billion?"

"Everybody knows him. I doubt he'd be interested in what you have to sell. But he should be here in the next hour."

"Is there a good place to get something to eat around here?"

"That bar across the way. It serves excellent meals."

"What do we ask for, fried larvae?"

One hour later the infamous Dinklet arrived at the booth. Talisa introduced herself to him. "I am 2N of 6 billion. You wanted to see me?"

"I have tirithium. One hundred per cent pure."

He garbled when he laughed. "No one has that."

"Test it and you'll agree."

The Dinklet led them into a two story cement building behind the booth where several armed guards watched over lab workers. "Let's see what you have?"

Golbot removed a vial from his coat and handed it over. The Dinklet examined it by eye and then poured out a small amount in a test tube. He placed it in a chamber and spun it around. When the data was revealed his eyes bulged out and saliva dripped from the side of his mouth. "Where did you get this?"

"Never mind that. Are you interested?"

"This quality is only available from the highest sources on Tiri. But yes, I am very interested. What is your price?"

"Information. You spent some time in prison with a cell mate named Andropodi?"

"He was a geologist. I had heard he escaped."

"We're interested in his whereabouts. That's our price."

The Dinklet hunched over. "I have no idea where he is. The last I saw of him was in jail."

"Another prisoner said you two were close. He said he confided in you. Maybe there is something you might remember?"

"We had many conversations. To tell you the truth, he was often incoherent. Confused." The Dinklet scraped his bristly arms together. "I remember now. He said something about going home."

Dr. Tralin glanced at the others. "To Benari?"

"No, it wasn't Benari. Now let me see, what did he say? No, it was Javensbee. I never heard of it."

Their heads drooped. "Of course."

"So do I get the tirithium?"

Golbot nodded. "All yours." They began to leave when Gobot swung around. "I wouldn't spread it around for a while. We stole it from one of the governors."

"Not to worry. By the time I dilute it, no one will ever know where it came from."

They boarded Talisa's ship. "When's the last time you went to Javensbee?" asked Golbot snidely.

Talisa entered the coordinates. "Five hundred years, or so."

Dr. Tralin was mystified. "It hasn't been called that in over eight hundred years. I believe it's now called Motinia."

"Why would he go there?"

"And why would he call it home?"

* *

The Chancellor's admirals had supplied a plan to invade the Fentelop system, a Makeo controlled territory comprised of sixteen solar systems with military and commercial operations. The Benarian D5 and E4 fleets surrounded the system and constricted the movements of the Makeo command. Unlike the Makeo, Benarian fleets had fewer ships but were more advanced. The Makeo outposts surrendered quickly and were given two weeks to evacuate.

The Chancellor met with his admirals. "The invasion has been a success. When can we remove the E4 fleet?"

"Within hours, Chancellor."

"Good. I want more contingency plans for future invasions. If Hecor continues to push us, we want to make it as unpalatable as possible."

"I agree. Hecor will not stop here. He is one determined megalomaniac."

"I still want to know one thing. If we engage the Makeo in all out war, can we ultimately triumph?"

"With all due respect, Chancellor. Define triumph?"

"Force Hecor to surrender."

"Our technology may prevail. But trillions would perish."

The Chancellor grimly soured. "That's what I thought. So it's time to call Hecor's bluff. We'll make a stand at Relemark. I'm no military genius, but even I can see that Relemark is the prize of the galaxy."

"Are we to invade Relemark?"

"Oh no, that would be all out war. Let's provide Hecor with a simple show of force at the outer perimeter. As many fleets as you can spare."

"I'll get right on it."

General Hecor gathered around his generals and contemplated the latest Benarian operations at Fentelop. His mood was jovial as he stuffed chunks of meat into his wide mouth. "So the Chancellor has won his first little battle?"

"The fool has no idea of what's coming."

"Let him have his temporary glory. Have you prepared the tenth fleet for the Ri system?"

"As you requested. Do you think the Chancellor will overreact? Ri is much closer to Benari space. But we do have the weapon."

"General, be patient. Having the weapon does not mean we want to use it right way. We want to rule the galaxy, not destroy it."

"My apologies, General Hecor."

"Have the tenth fleet stay clear of Ri. But make no mistake; I'm going to be much more aggressive in this system."

The Fentelop evacuation had continued at a brisk pace even as the Makeo tenth fleet had amassed near the Ri system. The Benari government compensated for this tactic by sending a small fleet of its own. Surprised by the small force against him, General Hecor had hoped for a more robust challenge. Ri was not only near Benari space, it had many popular vacation worlds, including the wooded planet that Dengy had often visited. Although the Benari fleet was small, they had enforcements near their space that outnumbered the Makeo tenth fleet. The Benari fleet took flank positions in front of the projected path of the tenth fleet.

Oribud had been summoned to Hecor's chambers. "You wish to see me?"

"I have a question about your weapon. I have seen what it can do to an entire planet, but I'm curious about its detonation capability in space; say between a Benari fleet?"

"How many vessels I can eliminate with a single weapon? I can destroy with one weapon any ships within a thousand mile radius."

Hecor's eyes bulged. "Remarkable. That is sufficient. I will be destroying several battle groups at once."

"Do you intend to destroy most of the fleet?"

"Once again, Oribud, you have overstepped your authority. But your response to my question has enlightened me."

"Again, I apologize for my presumptuousness."

"You're dismissed."

Lieutenant Fecan escorted Javensbee out of Hecor's chambers and down a long hallway. "So lieutenant, what do you think of our leader's strategy so far?"

"I never question the General."

"Come now, Fecan. I know your type. You can't really believe our general has acted as decisively as we would have."

"What I believe is none of your business, Oribud."

"But you must admit my weapon would end this war quickly?"

Fecan stopped. "If it were up to me, the Benari military would be completely destroyed. Is that what you want to hear?"

"We think alike."

Both forces remained motionless near the Ri system while the Benari military dispatched twenty impressive battle groups to the front edge of the Relemark system. It was well known that the government that controlled Relamark space with its valuable commercial assets would essentially control the power base of the galaxy. The Chancellor had gambled that it was still in the

Makeo's best interest to avoid all out war and felt vindicated when Hecor did not order an attack on the Benari.

* ** *

Talisa's ship reduced speed upon entry into Motinia's home star system. The planet, formally known as Javensbee, was the fifth body from its star. They slowed down considerably when the planet appeared in the view screen. Talisa notified the authorities and was directed to land at one of their three orbiting stations. Much like what the creators of Javensbee had originally intended; the planet's weather was now tamed with an abundance of greenery and fresh water.

Tralin put on his coat. "It's been so long."

"Let's go find Ceylar."

"I've arranged a meeting with a high official. It's still an advantage to be the respected Dr. Tralin of the Benari."

The ship was guided automatically into the docking area and they were shuttled to the capital city where they would meet the high commissioner. Impressed by the current geographical complexities of moist air, richly hued flowers and sweet nectar, they waited for the high commissioner in his office. "Dr. Tralin, I presume. My name is Commissioner Badua."

"Thank you for meeting us. These are my colleagues, Talisa Caru and Golbot."

"What can I do for you?"

"We're looking for a friend."

"Do you have a name? A bioscan?"

"His name is Andropodi, but we don't have a bioscan. We have a depiction."

The commissioner scanned the photo in his computer. After a few seconds, he gave it back to Tralin. "We don't have a match. Without a bioscan, it's could be very difficult to locate your friend. We have over three billion residents on this planet."

"Then we'll have to search for him. Our friend is an expert geologist. Perhaps that will narrow our search."

"I'll supply you with a list of our foundations and colleges."

"Thank you, Commissioner Badua. You have been very helpful."

They boarded a midsize commercial transport to the city where the most prestigious academy of geology was located. The city energy field was opened momentarily and the transport vessel landed at the main terminal. From there they departed on a smaller shuttle and landed near a college nestled inside an artificially constructed valley. They joined a stream of faculty and students wandering through its manicured gardens and towering trees.

The Dean, a busy humanoid, seemed inconvenienced by their arrival. "I must say, a simple bioscan would have saved time."

"We are aware of that, sir."

"Anyway, I don't know this friend of yours."

"Perhaps some of your professors may know him? He is well respected."

"I'll make some inquiries. But I can't guarantee anything."

Over the next two days they had meetings with several geologists, none of which could identify Dr. Ceylar. Before they departed they had a final meeting with the Dean, who gave them information about less prominent geological establishments. After visiting most of them, they still didn't find their friend.

* ** * *

The Benarians ordered their military forces to several other Makeo colonies. The Makeo forces near the Ri system had remained in neutral territory; however another nearby system, the Tobar collective, seem to be the target of a new Makeo advance. The Makeo fleet approached the Tobar system and the Benari only sent a small contingency of vessels to intercept them.

For the first time the Makeo forces entered a system and fired weapons on minimally guarded outposts, causing destruction and several deaths. The Benari forces were twenty minutes away and were unable to engage the Makeo. Vessels from within Tobar space tried to fend off the attack, but were instantly obliterated and sent off in flames. Just before the Benari arrived, the Makeo forces retreated back to the Ri system where they joined the main fleet.

The Benari fought valiantly, but much like at Tobar they were outnumbered and were defeated. By the time the Benari sent reinforcements, the Makeo had fled the Ri system. After the Benari regained control over both systems, they didn't pursue the Makeo. The Chancellor and his military advisors had been blindsided and humiliated. An emergency session was convened to ponder their future strategy.

"We should enter Relamark now."

The Chancellor tried to remain calm. "Admiral, this is exactly what Hecor wants us to do. He obviously desires war."

"The damage reports are in. Minor damage at Ri. More extensive at Tabor. Fifty personnel have been killed, twenty injured."

"This is cataclysmic. Our next decisions will affect everyone in the galaxy. Hecor has demonstrated he is a formidable foe. He wants war, he'll have war.

An aid burst into the room. "Hecor wants to speak with you."

"Put him on."

The General sat proudly at his desk. "So we have finally engaged."

"A surprise attack is beneath you, Hecor."

"That was practice. Besides, my forces aren't the ones gathered near the Relamark system."

"We haven't attacked anyone."

"In response to your obvious aggressive stance at Relemark, I believe its time to match your forces. I'm ordering twenty fleets to the perimeter."

"General, you can stop this now. Please consider a truce?"

"Goodbye, Chancellor."

Hecor turned to his general with glee. "He has no idea of what's to come."

"General Hecor, our public is weary."

"I'm confident we will have their support. Once we're at Relemark, I don't want any provocative moves. We must fortify our positions around the home world before we make that move. See to the reassignment of forces from Qetoriposute."

Eight fleets consisting of battle cruisers and a myriad of smaller attack vessels traveled synchronously towards the Relemark perimeter. The citizens of Relemark, sixty per cent of them Benarian, chattered nervously about the looming fleets gathering at the edges of system. Soon the Makeo fleets stretched across the entire border opposite the Benarian fleets at the other side of the system. Relemark now had the largest military forces assembled in over two hundred years.

* *

The three members of the Mist had visited most of the geological institutions on the planet and were unsuccessful in their attempt to find Dr. Ceylar. Frustrated, they began to search for him at remote geological dig sites. Standing in the ruins of a desert wasteland, Talisa began to erratically pace and wave her fists wildly. "We're going at this all wrong."

"What do you mean?"

"We're assuming Ceylar came here as a geologist. But Andropodi never lived on Javensbee. The Dinklet never mentioned he was going home to be a geologist."

"True, he has been regressing the whole time."

"He's demonstrating mental disability. He may not know who he is. That's why our bonding has been in vein."

They met again with Commissioner Badua. "Not having any luck finding your friend?"

"No, but we may have another theory. He may have become mentally impaired. We'd like to expand our search to mental facilities."

"That shouldn't be a problem. I will contact Hjurula. If your friend is at any of those facilities, she will know."

All was quiet in the Benari and Makeo ranks as they waited on opposite sides of the Relemark system. Although there was plenty of fear and indecision among the citizens, an evacuation order had not been announced by either side. And then without any warning the Makeo fleets moved slowly past the Relemark perimeter and the Chancellor and his admirals prepared for the worst.

"This is it. The invasion."

Another admiral seemed circumspect. "We should wait to see their intentions."

"I agree", responded the Chancellor. "Hecor is unpredictable. He may be baiting us. One thing for sure, we can not relinquish Relemark."

And then as suddenly as it began the Makeo forces halted in mid space and held their positions. Without any further provocation, the Benari fleet remained static and awaited orders from their command.

General Hecor delightfully gloated. "I knew they wouldn't send their forces at us. This Chancellor's advisors are extremely cautious."

"We should hit them with everything we've got."

"Patience, my friend. This is an art form. Enjoy the game. The Chancellor will probably be given the advice that as long our forces don't engage, they shouldn't respond. So our next move will be to give them a reason to attack."

"The weapon?"

"Yes, the weapon. Its time has come. I haven't decided what target I'm going to hit. But it will be decisive."

The Mist boarded a transport to the main mental facility on Motinia. Six guards led them through hallways where species, some humanoid, some multi-legged, some gelatinous and others with bright feathers were kept in secured confinement. They met with Hjurula. "Dr. Tralin, it is an honor to have you as my guest. I've been told that a friend of yours may be here?"

"We don't have a bioscan." He handed her the picture. "This is the best I can do. I hope you can find him."

She scanned her computer. "I'm sorry; nothing."

Tralin was disappointed. "What about other facilities?"

"There are only five on this planet and I've accessed them all."

Golbot interrupted. "How about regular hospitals?"

"I can scan them." She entered the photograph and thousands of faces passed over Dr. Ceylar's. It then stopped on a perfect match. "We have him. He's in a hospital in the northern region."

They could hardly contain their enthusiasm upon arriving at the hospital. They raced towards a resident female doctor who greeted them with much relief. "It just seemed like no one would ever claim patient 4587. He's been here for two years. We don't know anything about him."

"What's wrong with him?"

The doctor gestured for them to follow her. "We don't know. He's been in a coma. We tried to scan for brain activity, but our equipment could not penetrate. We even tried laser scalpels, but his skin is impervious."

Tralin nodded. "His name is Ceylar. And it would be difficult to explain his existence. But I believe we can facilitate your scans."

She escorted them down several corridors past successive rooms until they arrived at Dr. Ceylar's room where he peacefully rested on a bed surrounded by medical equipment. He was the same tall, gaunt, dark skinned, bald headed friend with a strip of beard stretching ear to ear. Tralin stroked his forehead. "And now we know the reason we could not contact him."

"How is this possible, Tralin?"

"I don't know, Golbot. But we're going to find out. Doctor, prepare your scans. I think you will get a reading now." He placed his hand over Ceylar's chest and a purplish glow illuminated his body. Much to her surprise, the doctor began receiving data on his condition.

"He's Benarian. Vital signs are excellent. Oh no, here's the problem. His brain activity is severely restricted. There's much damage. He's suffering from a disease known as Latodolophon Riolisis. It's rare, but not totally uncommon. We have other patients with the same disease."

"What's the cure?"

Her head swayed forlornly. "There is no cure."

"Not even with today's technology?"

"I'm afraid there is no hope for your friend. He will remain in this coma until he dies."

Talisa pounded bed sheets. "Die? He can't die."

The doctor stared oddly at Talisa and then the lights in the room flickered. The floor rumbled gently at first and then the equipment rattled more intensely. In the corner of the room a figure took shape and within seconds the Songster materialized. Shocked, the doctor ran towards the door when Tralin stopped her. "It's okay. We know him. But we'd like to be alone with him."

"Of...course. But if you need me, I'll be outside."

The songster clapped his hands giddily, then frenetically. "Congratulations! You found the great Dr. Ceylar. Now you know what I know. And I only had to help you once to get here. I was the Dinklet's jail mate."

"What did you do to him?"

"Do to him? I did nothing to him. That's the beauty of this. You can blame my creators. They did this to him. That perfect race of beings that could do no wrong. Or so it seemed."

"This is impossible."

"My creators gave the Mist immortality in order to frustrate my ambitions. Only they missed something. With all their

97

expert scientific abilities, they made a mistake. They were flawed. It's that simple. They missed something in Ceylar's genetics. You see Latodolophon Riolisis is identical to Alterium Riolisis in its early stages. The later being common and easily treated. This little disease remains dormant, but can be activated in later life. Such as the case with Dr. Ceylar."

"So the only question is why haven't you taken over the galaxy? I mean, using General Hecor as a pawn seems ridiculous."

"You don't understand. If my creators can make a mistake, then I can make a mistake. And if one can make a mistake, then one has the ability to fix that mistake. Don't you see Talisa? I'm not just hopeless evil minded creation. I can change."

"You really want me? That's what this is all about?"

"You don't believe me, and I understand that. But in time you will see that I have changed. My creators thought I was an error; an abomination. I am going to prove them wrong once again. Until Ceylar's coma, I thought I was hopeless. But now I can learn from my mistakes to improve myself." He gazed upon Ceylar. "I only wish I could kill him for you. But he is immortal, doomed to an eternity of silence. For that, my creators did more damage to him than I ever could have."

Talisa twisted her fingers throughout her flowing white hair. "I don't understand this, Javensbee? If this is to impress me, then stop this war now?"

He stared endearingly. "End this war? It is for this reason that I started it. I knew that the prospect of the Makeo ruling the galaxy was particularly repulsive to you. After all, they killed your mother and father so many years ago."

"I've forgiven them for that."

"Talisa, you will be at my side sooner or later. That's what this is all about. But you must come to this decision on your own. When you realize that the Mist is finished, then you will come to me willingly. At this moment you still have hope that something can be done for Ceylar. As long as you are convinced of that, you will never be mine."

Golbot stood in between them. "All right, Javensbee. You've had your say. Now leave us."

He threw up his hands. "My pleasure. I'm wanted on the Makeo battlefield." He dissipated into a fog and drifted out of the room.

"We're in big trouble."

Dr. Tralin clutched onto Talisa's arms. "It all makes sense now."

"What?"

"Javensbee was telling the truth. He really does love you."

"You're crazy."

"Think about it. He's known about Ceylar all this time. If he didn't want to convince you of his sincerity, he would have just taken Ceylar to some distant planet and buried him deep inside. We may have never found him. Or better, just send him flying out the galaxy all together."

"I see your point."

"And this is our only advantage. As long as Javensbee desires you, we have time to figure this out. But just in case he does change his mind, let's implant sub-dermal tracking devices." Tralin summoned the doctor. "We'd like to transport our friend to Benari."

"I'll will make the arrangements." She looked around the room. "And your other friend?"

"He had to go."

SIX

THE MAKEO FLEET REMAINED MOTIONLESS within the boundaries of Relemark space. Uncertain of their next move, the Benari command was on constant alert for a surprise attack. Without warning a Makeo battle cruiser with its smaller support vessels moved swiftly towards a Benarian military space station. They surrounded the orbiting complex but did not make any provocative moves. The Benarian commander contacted the home world which instructed him only to defend the station if necessary.

All was silent until the battle cruiser unleashed a volley of low yield missiles that wore down the station's shields. Benarian fighters emerged from the docks and were intercepted by numerous Makeo fighters. The Benari vessels were easily disabled and the battle cruiser began to shoot holes into the side of the station. The commander surrendered immediately, but not before thirty crew members were either killed or injured. The Benarian Chancellor gave the order for his fleet to invade the Relemark system and pursue the Makeo in battle.

The Chancellor sat grimly along side his admirals. "War has begun. Hecor has made the decision for all of us."

"It was always his intention."

"It's a sad day for the galaxy. Billions, perhaps trillions may lose their lives."

"We had no choice, Chancellor. We can not back down."

An aide to the Chancellor walked over to him. "Excuse me, sir, but Dr. Tralin would like to address the council."

"Tralin?"

"He says it's a matter of national security."

"This is highly unusual. But his reputation precedes him. Show him in."

Tralin rushed over to the long table. "Forgive me for the intrusion. But it is necessary that you halt the fleet."

"Are you mad?"

"No, I am not. If you engage the Makeo, your forces will be destroyed."

"Our fleet is more than enough for them."

"You don't understand. The Makeo have a weapon. It's like none you have ever witnessed. There is no defense against it. Hecor wants this engagement."

"How do you know about this weapon? We have heard rumors, but nothing substantiated."

"A Galconian trader sold it to him. The weapon is real."

"I can't just stop the fleet on your word."

"All I'm asking you is to send one automated battle cruiser with a small battle group ahead of the main fleet."

"Hecor's sensors will detect the lack of crew."

"Talisa Caru has a technology that fools her enemy into believing there's a full crew on board. We can install it on your cruiser."

The Chancellor balked. "I don't know…"

"Please, if I'm right it may save countless lives."

The Benari fleet traveled unabated on their journey across Relemark to meet the Makeo, who were still motionless near their side of the boarder. The Benari then unexplainably slowed down to a stop, befuddling Hecor and his generals. A single battle cruiser group pulled out ahead of the fleet and continued towards the Makeo. "What are they doing", asked one of Hecor's generals.

"He entangled his boney fingers together. "They're testing us. They don't have the stomach for all out war."

"What should we do?"

"Nothing. Let them come. Tell Oribud his first target is on the way."

The Benarian battle cruiser and support group slowed down and stopped in front of the wall of Makeo vessels. The cruiser was scanned and it was verified as being fully staffed according to Makeo sensors. The battle cruiser shot a barrage of torpedoes at the line of Makeo ships and then Javensbee, in the form of a single missile, detonated in a blinding white heat that eliminated the Benari battle group.

The Chancellor and his admirals were horrified and knew a weapon of this magnitude would leave them defenseless in all future battles. Dr. Tralin had given them good advice and now it was up to the Chancellor to ask Hecor for terms of surrender. Hecor sat with his generals, hardly able to withhold his composure. "I realize that the Benari feel entitled to conditions of surrender, but I will offer none."

"This weapon of yours is genocidal. Even a great military leader as you would never use it against innocent civilians."

"I will use all methods to ensure your cooperation, Chancellor. And to assure your cooperation I'm going to give you a little demonstration of what this weapon can really do. I am sending a small contingency of ships to the moon, R4679. It's a mining operation of yours. We will evacuate the miners and then eliminate the moon."

"Is that really necessary?"

"Oh, yes it is. And then we will talk surrender."

General Hecor was true to his word. The miners were evacuated in eight hours and the galaxy all watched the lead Makeo battle cruiser move into proximity of the tiny satellite.

A missile was fired that impacted the surface and exploded huge chunks of dirt and rocks in every direction; eventually ripping the moon apart in so many pieces it drifted off as an asteroid field.

The Makeo then proceeded through Relemark toward Benari space and the Chancellor communicated with Hecor. "We will comply with your terms of surrender?"

"Chancellor, it is not my intention to rule the galaxy with totalitarianism. Your leaders will resume positions in government and only serve me as a benevolent tyrant, as it were. As long as your citizens hold to my laws, and these laws will not be too intrusive, you will be able to live as you always have. This is not the end of the galaxy, but the beginning of a new era."

"Thank you. I am grateful."

"Of course you must reduce your military by half. I will deliver some coordinates where your ships will be space docked. The remainder of your fleet will patrol as usual. The assignments will be relayed to your admirals."

"Thank you, General. You are a gracious conqueror."

"I will be personally visiting you in my cruiser next month; or perhaps sooner, for the formal declaration of surrender. It will be the crowning event in this historic new world order."

Hecor ended the transmission and Javensbee walked into the room. "You wish to see me, General?"

"Yes, Oribud. I just wanted to congratulate you on your efficiency. The weapon has performed beyond my expectations. It also begs the question, is Oribud of Galcon satisfied with his position, or does he want more?"

Javensbee almost closed one eye. "Are you suggesting a power play on my part?"

"The thought has come to mind. After all, you have the power."

"General, as I stated before, I'm here to serve you and the Makeo Empire. I am loyal to my Galcon ancestry. I seek nothing more than my commission."

"You've earned my gratitude, Oribud. This victory of ours will live through our peoples forever. Galcon has been vindicated."

* *

While many in the galaxy were beginning to digest the loss of freedom, Dr. Tralin had invited some of the most respected brain specialists to his Benarian estate. He rested comfortably on a couch surrounded by the scientists. "Ladies and gentlemen, you have seen the data. You have examined the patient. Is there anything you see here that indicates these findings can be reversed?"

"There is no question he is suffering from Latodolophon Riolisis. And I'm afraid that disease is incurable. That is unfortunately the collective opinion of all science on this subject."

"It is difficult for me to accept that any disease is incurable."

"We have done much experimentation with this type of brain degradation and have never produced results. It is an inevitable conclusion when one is dealing with the mind and its complex structure. We know so much about it, and yet there is so much more we need to know. I fear we have failed you."

"Failure in this case is not an option."

"None the less, you as a scientist must realize there are certain limitations with any technology. We have such a quandary."

"Dr. Tralin, you should just allow your friend to pass on with dignity."

"Pass on? If you only knew."

"I would be happy to study this data once more, if that would help. Maybe there is something we missed."

"Thank you, doctor."

"Perhaps all of us could do the same?"

"I appreciate all your help. Thank you for coming."

General Hecor had given the order to disperse the Makeo military forces into all regions of the galaxy. He had been true to his word and refrained from attacking any more military and civilian targets. Although many cultures were still suspicious of Makeo motives, they resumed their normal territorial patrolling duties. The Benari also cooperated by mooring half their fleet in the designated areas as dictated by Makeo command.

The average citizens went about their normal routines, trading and making profits as they had been doing for centuries. There were skirmishes with the Makeo, but most of the governments were quick to diffuse escalating confrontations. Others complained in courts, but were usually rebuffed by the new Makeo bylaws.

Once the Makeo had secured the Relemark system they could now profit from the lucrative benefits the region offered. To the Chancellor's ire, many of the Benarian military bases in the Relemark, as well as others in the distant regions were slowly taken over by the Makeo. There were some dissension among Benarian military leaders, but they were immediately arrested and sent to prison camps.

As the Makeo solidified their control over one territory, they methodically moved into another. It was only now that most citizens began to feel the full impact of the new rule of law. Hecor had given them autonomy, but the price was loyalty and subservience to a way a life completely foreign to them. Back on the Benarian home world preparations began for the grand arrival of General Hecor and his entourage.

Even more troubling were the orders given to Benarian Admirals from lesser officers in the Makeo military. Although Hecor insisted on respect, many of the Makeo officers delighted in their new authority and tried to humiliate their counterparts. Sometimes there were violent confrontations between Benarian and Makeo military personnel, resulting in brutal retaliation that led to execution. The Chancellor would complain about the unfair treatment, but general Hecor would often dismiss it outright.

Much better was the treatment of the ordinary citizen that enjoyed protection from Hecor and his courts. The Makeo were given training and advice on how to handle disputes among the other races. Hecor was determined to allow prosperity to flourish among those of the merchant class.

On the Benarian home world Dr. Tralin, Talisa and Golbot gathered at Tralin's estate. Downtrodden and frustrated, they tried to reach a consensus as Ceylar rested motionless in one of the bedrooms. Talisa stared at the medical evidence on the monitor. "The though of spending eternity with the Songster is repugnant."

Golbot chuckled. "I'm glad it's you, not me."

"I guess that saving the galaxy is a worthwhile objective."

"That's assuming Javensbee has really changed."

With desperate inevitability, Talisa sought Dr. Tralin's advice. "Should I give into the enemy?"

He covered his face with both hands. "That prospect seems untenable. Still, we must face the fact that Ceylar may never recover. Can you imagine that, an endless coma? What horror. What absolute horror."

"Then I really have no choice."

Tralin's thoughts were preoccupied with the monitor screen that contained Ceylar's medical charts. He was about to answer Talisa when he noticed something very familiar. He wasn't certain, but there was something in the brain wave patterns that he may have missed the first time. There was a familiarity that he could not explain. "Wait just now. This may be something."

"What do you see?"

"I wonder? This can't be. I've seen these brain patterns before. For the life of me, I don't know where."

"I don't know how? We just found Ceylar."

"No, it's not that." He snapped his fingers. "Of course! A young scientist of mine. He was working on a project with very similar patterns."

"Who is he?"

"He and his wife were transferred somewhere. It shouldn't

be difficult to trace him down. He might just be the one to help us."

Dengy was alone in his apartment while his wife was at work finishing her military project assignment. His hair was unkempt, his whiskers overgrown and his apparel was messy and stained. He shuffled aimlessly from room to room until a message alerted him that Dr. Tralin was contacting him. He hastily brushed his fingers through his hair before Tralin appeared on the monitor.

"Dengy, it's good to see you."

"It's an honor."

"How are you and Ale doing?"

"We're doing just fine. She's expecting in four months."

He paused. "I hope I'm not imposing on you, but I need a favor. Can you come to my estate?"

"Yeah, sure. Ale has a little more clean up, but I can be there in three days."

"It's important."

General Hecor met with Javensbee and Lieutenant Fecan in his office. "Oribud, I am going to be traveling to Benari in my personal battle cruiser. Fecan has my security, but you must guarantee the fleet's security."

"You have my word, General."

"I don't expect an attack, but just in case I want to respond by destroying their home world."

"I'm prepared to follow your orders."

"And you Fecan, I'm entrusting you with my life."

"I will select the guards myself."

Hecor was neatly groomed for his first official ceremony from the balcony of the great hall; a multi-colored structure of twisting arches and tinted glass. Tens of thousands of Makeo citizens stood shoulder to shoulder waiting for words from their new leader. Makeo music, ugly and monotone by most standards, echoed throughout the kingdom. They clapped and shouted until their leader silenced them with a hand gesture. "Citizens of Makeo, we understand the struggles of those that came before us." The hall vibrated with loud stomping feet. "I was once your General. I am now your devoted supreme leader. I will be leaving for the Benari home world with a message of conquest and hope for the entire galaxy. This is a time for all Makeo to rejoice that we have taken our place as the greatest empire ever known. I promise to lead you to the best of my ability and crush those enemies that may try to stop us. Living in fear of the Benari is no longer tolerated. We are the victors!"

* *

Dengy arrived by transport to the Benari home world and then boarded a shuttle to Dr. Tralin's front lawn. Still curious about his summons, Dengy tugged and adjusted his pants and straightened out his shirt. He passed through a short hallway into the living room, which always had the whiff of freshly cut flowers.

Tralin embraced him. "Dengy, thank you for coming."

"Have you been reinstated?"

"No, I am still retired. I asked you to come here for a very specific reason. I need you to look over some medical information." He herded Dengy over to the monitor screen on his desk. "What does this look like to you?"

"Neurological strands, brain wave patterns. Lower brain synapses. These readings show an extremely damaged brain."

"It's called Latodolophon Riolisis. It's a rare disease."

"I've heard of it. I believe this disease is Incurable?"

"So I've been told."

"Excuse me for asking, but who is this?"

"A friend. Do you notice anything else about these patterns?"

"I'm not a doctor. I'm a scientist. But it is obvious that your patient's lower brain functions have been severely damaged. It's difficult for me to say from these images. I assume he is in a coma?"

Tralin turned away from Dengy. "You don't recognize the patterns, do you?"

Dengy nodded. "Yes, I do. They are similar to what I was experimenting with before my work was cancelled."

"Do you think you might be able to cure him?"

Dengy's body became rigid. "Now wait a minute. My work was in its early stages. Trials weren't scheduled for years."

"I didn't ask you that. Can you cure him?"

"Even if I could, it's never been tried on a living person. I could damage him further, or even kill him. I can't risk that."

Tralin sighed and sat down on the edge of his desk. "I'm going to ask you a strange question. Do you believe in the story about the Songster of Javensbee?"

"Why would you ask that?"

"I'm curious. Do you believe it's real, or a myth?"

Embarrassed, Dengy's shoulders swayed. "Come on, Dr. Tralin. You're talking about a kid's story."

"Am I? What if I told you that you had an ancestor that had seen the Songster and met a group called the Mist?"

"How did you know that?"

"What if I were to tell you it's all true?"

Dengy chuckled nervously. "This seems a little out of character for you."

"Come with me, Dengy." He walked out onto the balcony and stood against the rail. Without warning, he fell backwards over the rail and bounced down the cliff side to the river below. Tongue bitten, throat swollen, tears flowing, Dengy backed away from the rail and slammed himself against the wall of the house. Before he could utter a word, he snapped out of it and went to call the authorities. As quick as that thought entered his mind, Talisa's ship hovered ten feet off the balcony with the side door opened to reveal a smiling Dr. Tralin. The side of the ship lifted over the rail and Tralin jumped down on the balcony floor. When the ship banked and jetted away, Dengy stood numb with mouth agape while Dr. Tralin dusted off his clothes.

"I'm sorry I had to be so dramatic. I could have just shot myself in the head with a laser, but I wanted to demonstrate that this was no trick."

"The Mist is real? The stories my ancestor told were true?"

"How did you think General Hecor has been so successful? Javensbee has been manipulating him, as well as all of us."

Dengy pointed back into the living room. "And your friend with the brain disease is also one of the Mist?"

"Yes. And without him, we can not expel the Songster. You see Dengy, I knew your ancestor and I knew you were related to him before I hired you. I thought it was a grand gesture for a very brave friend so long ago. Little did I know that you may be exactly what we need."

"This science of mine is in its infancy."

Talisa and Golbot entered the living room and were introduced to him. Dr. Tralin put his hand on his shoulder. "Dengy, you may be our only hope. The doctor's have stated that this disease is irreversible."

Dengy exhaled. "I was beginning to think this was a dream. Okay, it's possible I might be able to repair enough neuron strands to communicate with your friend. But that's pretty basic stuff from where I left off."

"It's a start."

Dengy paced around the room. "I'll need my old equipment, and a L416 virtual processor. And my wife to assist me."

"I can arrange a lab at the institution. I still have enough clout to procure a L416. I believe there are three units on Benari. I'll make a personal plea to the Chancellor."

Golbot spoke up. "There's one more thing, young scientist. Nobody can know about this. Nobody outside this room, with the exception of your wife."

"He's right, Dengy. The Songster must be left in the dark."

Dengy held out his hands. "I don't know if I can even contact your friend. The person you know may not even exist any longer."

"That's always a possibility. But we have to try." Tralin turned to Talisa. "You'd better go. You know what you have to do."

* *

Talisa set a course to intercept General Hecor's battle cruisers on their way to Benari space. It only required two days travel to reach him. A crew member on Hecor's cruiser alerted him of a small vessel approaching their coordinates. They reduced to sub-light speed and Hecor personally addressed the occupant of the familiar ship. "Talisa Caru, what business do you have with me?"

"Hello General, it's been a while. I understand you have a Galcon trader named Oribud on board?"

"You know him?"

"We're old friends. May I speak with him?"

Hecor summoned Javensbee to the bridge. "How do you know this mercenary?"

"We are acquaintances."

"She would like to speak with you." Hecor signaled his communications officer. "Bring her up on the screen."

She smiled. "Hello Oribud. You're looking well."

"As are you."

"I need to see you. Can you come over?"

"I'm certain that can be arranged."

Javensbee went to the transporter room and beamed over to Talisa's ship. Confident and full of bravado, he sat down next to her in the co-pilot's chair. "Well, well, here you are. Coming to me this time."

She smiled with a squint in her greenish blue eyes. "You were right about everything. There is nothing we can do for Ceylar."

"This is the opinion of your experts?"

"That's why I'm here. So what's next?"

"I have a retreat. A beautiful place. We shall go there."

"What about your General?"

111

"I'll tell him I need a little time off. I'll assure him the missiles are armed. I'm certain he will spare me for a few days."

Hecor wasn't too pleased, but felt he owed Javensbee a young woman's overture. He reluctantly allowed them to depart once assurances were given that the missiles were armed. Once on board Talisa'a ship she asked him for the coordinates of his estate. "I have a small place in the Ri system." He prepared to snap his fingers and she grabbed his hand .

"Wait, Javensbee. I'll take us there the old fashion way."

"The old fashioned way? How arcane."

"That's the way I want it. If I'm to be your lover and companion, I want to live as normal a life as possible."

Resigned, he slumped back into the co-pilot's chair. "Then by all means…"

Two days later they arrived in the Ri system, where they flew past three planets and fifteen moons before angling towards the dark side of a small planet with a bright moon. They pierced through the atmosphere and circled the planet a few times before heading in the direction of a towering mountainous expanse. It was dark with only the moon and a smattering of lights below to guide their way. Javensbee's retreat came into view on a flattened plateau between four high mountain peaks. The one story rectangular structure had sharp edges and glass walls on all sides with garden paths surrounding jutting observation decks.

Talisa steered the ship towards the front lawn and landed on a designated pad that lowered into the ground. "How did you acquire this place?"

"The former owner insisted."

"I'll bet."

They disembarked at the lowest of the three underground levels and entered a foyer with an elevator. They rode the elevator up to the top floor where the main room was decorated with luxurious wood, stone and soft fabric laden furniture strewn around a central fountain with exotic female statues. Javenbsee operated a control unit that darkened the clear glass walls into an opaque shine and dimmed the soft yellow, red and blue lights. Admiring the architecture, Talisa rested comfortably on a couch, unzipped her boots, tossed them on the floor and stretched out her legs on the cushions.

"You look beautiful, Talisa. And to think after these thousand years we are alone together."

"I must admit, it feels right for the wrong reasons."

"You have saved your precious galaxy."

She barely smiled. "I wouldn't go that far."

"Are you hungry?"

"What a strange question? I can eat food and I like it. But you and I don't need food to survive."

"I find eating a pleasure."

"I'm not here to eat" She stood up and draped her arms over his shoulders and around his back. "It's you that I want." She kissed him gently on the lips and then pressed harder against his mouth. They embraced fully in the middle of the room. "Now that's better than any food, uhh Javensbee?"

"It's odd, yet enticing."

She smiled. "They'll be a lot more of that. Are there any clothes in this place?"

"There are some women's things in the bedrooms on the floor below. Perhaps you can find something there."

She kissed him quickly and rode the elevator to one of the bedrooms where she found a suitable loose fitting night gown. She returned to Javensbee, who ran his palms up and down her shoulders and kissed her skin moistly. Talisa's body tingled with anticipation as he stroked her hair and arms with greater intensity, leading her over to a lengthy couch and pulling her gown up and over her head.

Naked and desirously vulnerable, she fell to the couch and he advanced slowly over her warm flesh, touching her sensitively along her thighs. He used both arms to propel himself off her body and looked directly into her eyes. "I am all the elements of nature and more. I will use my talents to please the one I have always loved."

"I'm all yours."

His lower torso and legs changed into circulating water, yet without the sensation of wetness. The watery flow cascaded over her legs and stomach as she clenched her fists unable to restrain the erotic stimulation. She grabbed his arms and tried to repel him when the sexual arousal was almost unbearable, but he persisted more. As the pressure of water circulation swirled against her, soft moans turned to loud ones. With no place to go, she screamed and screamed until it was all over for her. She had been reduced to a quivering balled up lump on the couch.

Javensbee reformed into his solid body. "Was I sufficient?"

She found little strength to slap him on top of the head. "How could you do that to me?"

"We're you not pleased?"

"Pleased? I have never had such an experience."

"I can repeat it now."

"No! Not for a while. I need to rest. Regain my senses."

He smiled. "If you have been satisfied, then I surely am satisfied at what has transpired here."

"Did you feel anything, Javensbee?"

"Does that matter?"

"It does to me."

"If you are asking if I had some kind of intense sexual experience…no. Not as you apparently have had. Perhaps that will come in time. However, knowing that I pleased you has delighted me."

"That's a start." She looked away from him. "Do you mind if we use one of those bedrooms down there to sleep for a while?"

"Talisa, neither of us needs to sleep."

"On the contrary we have taught ourselves to sleep. It oddly refreshes the mind. Beside, you'd better learn that a girl loves to cuddle."

He feigned nonchalantly. "Oh…"

She located the master bedroom, pulled down the sheets and crawled into bed. True to her word she nuzzled up to him.

"Do you think the Mist will ever accept us?"

She stretched her arm out over his chest. "Before this, I didn't think I would. But to answer your question, I don't know. You're the enemy, Javensbee. We can't let go of that so easily."

"Yet you can see yourself doing that very thing?"

"It's a paradox. But maybe one day we can understand your repentance. For the time being we are still trying to figure out how to save Dr. Ceylar. When that becomes futile, maybe they'll come around."

"I can't blame them for trying to save him."

She sat up. "Javensbee, I'm impressed. That was almost noble of you."

The following day Javensbee rejoined General Hecor and Talisa met with Dr. Tralin and Golbot. "What kind of progress are your having, Tralin?"

"Dengy is setting up the lab."

"That's it? Come on, you have to resolve this."

"Having problems with Javensbee?"

She exhaled with a lost stare. "You don't understand. This creature is an incredible lover. It's overwhelming."

Golbot laughed. "Get a hold of yourself, Caru. It's just a job."

She smacked him on the arm. "Just a job? He took me places I would never allow anyone else. I may have trouble controlling my emotions."

"Then you're going to have to learn how. We're depending on you. We still don't know if we can even reach Ceylar."

"You better, soon. I can't take much more of this."

"I'm confident Dengy can help us. You'll just have to hang on."

"Hang on to what?"

Tralin held her tightly by the arms. "Talisa, everybody in this whole damn galaxy is counting on you."

"Okay, I'll play the doting girlfriend. But you'd better get some results soon before I actually fall in love with him."

"He's that good?"

Later on Javensbee and Talisa reunited at the mountaintop estate where she hovered naked in mid-air over the living room floor. Javensbee as a warm vaporous cloud spun her around slowly and she screamed in ecstasy while he relentlessly pleased her. Her skin vibrated at every passing movement and she unsuccessfully begged him to stop. He set her down gently on the floor and she curled up into herself, gasping what air she could let in.

He rematerialized into his humanoid form and noticed she was crying. "What's wrong? Have I offended you?"

She wiped her tears. "You really don't understand."

"Then you are happy?"

"I'll say one thing, you're a wonderful lover. But please stop when I say stop!"

SEVEN

MUCH TO THE NEW DIRECTOR'S consternation, the Chancellor had personally requested that Dr. Tralin be assigned a new laboratory and the necessary tools and equipment to begin the experiment. Ale was thrilled to be working with her husband and was given the task to bring the systems up to fully operational. Dr. Ceylar silently rested on a special table that could be rolled out under the sophisticated surgical devices and the L416 virtual processor.

General Hecor had arrived in Benari space and prepared to receive the Chancellor as his guest on the lead battle cruiser. The voluminous Makeo fleet of twenty battle cruisers stretched across a vast territory of space. This relatively small armada was not intended to protect Makeo interests, but was intended to demonstrate the kind of power that would be spoken throughout the centuries. Accompanied by thirty of his aides and military commanders, the Chancellor beamed aboard Hecor's cruiser and was saluted by a long line of Makeo guards. The Chancellor met with Hecor in the large conference room where a few of his aides and his highest ranking admirals sat next to him. The event would be broadcasted to all the galaxy's citizens.

Hecor and his generals sat across from the Chancellor. Hecor

117

addressed the monitor screen. "We are here to commemorate the once proud Benari Empire and its compliance to the terms of surrender so prescribed. They have fought well, but have succumbed to a superior force. This does not mean we shall treat them like an inferior adversary. On the contrary, the Benari will continue to serve the Makeo as an example of our benevolence. I will now allow the Chancellor to speak."

"Thank you, General Hecor. And it is now my understanding that you shall be addressed as the Supreme Leader. On behalf of the Benarian Empire, I do so with my authority surrender to the Makeo. It has been a difficult time for us, but the war is over. It is also within my authority to comply with all Makeo tenants and law which will be judiciously followed by our civilian and military establishments. We have begun the docking of half of our fleet as directed and should be in compliance within a month."

"Thank you, Chancellor. Let me just say that you and your staff have been quite gracious. And I will try to fulfill my pledge of autonomy to your citizens. There may be times when we will have to arbitrate a dispute, but we hope that for the most part you will be able to govern yourselves. This is the beginning of a new era for all."

The broadcast was terminated and Hecor invited the Chancellor to tour his cruiser; a task that totally disgusted him. The Chancellor did not wish to offend General Hecor so he accepted the invitation and for the next few hours he inspected the troops and pretended to admire the ship's technology.

Dengy had installed all the equipment in the laboratory and prepared to run a series of tests. He had reviewed the material accumulated prior to the termination of his experiments and was now familiar with the new components. Ale followed up on the tests and validated that the system was operating at peak efficiency. Dengy seemed apprehensive, but Ale was more positive, unwilling to accept a society where her children would be raised in fear.

Dr. Ceylar was placed under the operating equipment; his

head directly under the surgical module. Dengy stood behind the main control panel and Ale sat next to him in front of six monitor stations. Dr. Tralin and Golbot were poised on each side of Ceylar and transferred their energy into his body to allow Dengy to proceed with the operation.

"I'm in. Twenty neural strands are misaligned. Twelve are damaged. I'm going to try to repair and seal one and see what happens." He turned to Ale. "Watch the heat signature carefully. If we destroy one, I want to calibrate fast."

"I'm on it."

He peeked around the control panel. "Dr. Tralin, this is the first time anyone has ever attempted this. We should be able to still communicate with him even if we lose some of the patterns."

"There's no other option. Proceed."

Dengy activated the cells and delivered energy pulses through the strands; a process necessary to interact with the pattern structure to rebuild brain material. Though it began to restructure the cells, the heat signature began to rise and burn off the exterior surface. Before it could permanently damage the material, the sealing process protected it. Ale was just about to claim victory when the energy pulses fluctuated and destabilized. "We're losing it."

"That's what I was afraid of. And this is the easiest process."

"We've stabilized again. All readings normal."

Dengy powered down. "We did it. The repair was successful."

"What does that mean?" asked Golbot.

Ale joyfully spun in her chair. "That means it's no longer theory. My husband has been vindicated."

"Let's not get overconfident. The more difficult repairs are coming next. We can repair, but can the repair suffice as a conduit for brain activity?"

Dr. Tralin put his hand on Ceylar's chest. "There's only one way to find out."

119

They initialized the next sequence of events and were dismayed when the repaired strand was damaged irreparably. The next few tries also resulted in failure and it soon became apparent to Dengy that they may lose all ability to communicate with Ceylar. He was dismayed. "I'm going to neglect the heat signature and activate the cells in one quick burst of energy. If I can keep ahead of the damn thing, it may seal cold before any permanent damage."

He proceeded and to his amazement and relief, the cell activity flourished before the heat could destroy it. The seal cohesively bonded and the patterns were now restored to normal. Ale jumped out of her chair. "We did it!"

Dengy almost collapsed on the control panel. "We did."

"Let's finish this" Golbot insisted.

An hour later they had repaired all the remaining communication patterns and were now ready to calibrate the L416 virtual processor. In their quest to save Ceylar, Dengy had cured Latodolophon Riolisis; something that all the great scientists were unable to achieve.

"What's next", asked Tralin.

"We have to connect the neuron links directly to the processor. That will allow us to actually communicate with Ceylar; if indeed that's still possible. We have to remember that he must have some level of consciousness."

"I have to believe he is still with us."

* *

At the first light of morning Talisa stood at the garden's edge and inhaled the cold dewy air. It was peacefully silent as the sun rose and painted the mountainside across from her. The warmth finally reached her face and she closed her eyes to enjoy its tranquil effects. Javensbee surprised her from behind and slipped his arm around her waist and stomach. She covered her hand over his. "You're appreciating the view? Your beauty even exceeds the very nature we see before us."

She smiled and pressed his hand against her stomach. "You have style, Javensbee. I'll give you that."

"I did not think it possible, but I am developing an emotionally attachment to you."

"I think the feeling's mutual. And that surprises me most of all."

His kissed her hair. "I am going to take you to a very special place." He held up his arm. "And don't argue with me."

"Where do you have in mind?"

"A planet at the far end of your galaxy. It's uninhabited and possesses a unique internal landscape."

"Lead the way."

He touched her shoulder and within seconds they vanished and reappeared inside a dark cave. It was pitch black and then with a swoop of Javensbee's hand the cave lit up in a blue phosphorous light and revealed fifty foot high quartz pillars and smooth cathedral like stalactites and stalagmites. A cool frost gathered around her nostrils. "Just how deep are we?"

"Ten miles below the surface of this planet. I came upon it by accident in my travels. It is one of the most impressive natural wonders I have ever seen."

She gazed upward. "I have to agree. It's so big in here. I've seen decorative caves, but this one is quite amazing."

"I brought you here for a very specific reason."

"Why, is sex in a cave something special?"

He laughed heartily. "No, but I'm going to show you something I haven't done, or wanted to do since the day I left my home planet. I'm going to play music for you. And you alone."

She stared intriguingly. "It was said that your music was breathtaking."

"My earliest talent." He held out his arms. "I just haven't had a reason until meeting you, Talisa."

"I'm honored."

He formed into a cloud and then vanished and the cave

suddenly lit up in sparkling yellow flashes. The floor shook with powerful vibrations and then Javensbee bounced a series of musical notes against the opposing cave walls and produced a percussive rhythm against the rocky surfaces. The notes became faster and were soon joined by a myriad of color trails tracing their journey across the cave surfaces. A lattice of colorful beams stretched from end to end, playing spectacular musical phrases that combined every tone imaginable.

Talisa gazed with fascination as the cone shaped stalactites chimed a counterpoint melody; each lit in a different color in syncopation with the crossing beams. Pow, pow, ping, pow, the notes dashed across the walls playing a style of music that she had never heard before. The stalactites turned silver and gold, bright as the sun at times, signaling a new thunderous round of bass notes from the stalagmites below. Every part of the cave was alive with melody, harmony and rhythm and every possible hue scattered in joyous concert with the music.

Just as suddenly as it began, the gold and silver stalactites seized playing, the beams of light dissipated and the only sound left was the thumping stalagmites on the cave floor. When it stopped, the cave was silent with a yellow afterglow. Javensbee reformed into his humanoid figure and she walked over to him and kissed him fervently. "That was remarkable."

"I wanted you to experience who I am."

"It was...I can't describe it. You should share it with others."

"Perhaps there will be a day."

"Me, I can't play a lick of music."

"You have other talents, Talisa."

* *

General Hecor's fleet was scheduled to remain in Benari space for a week's visit. He still had logistical arrangements to finalize, as well as some gloating before taking on the perks of a supreme ruler. He had accomplished dominance in a galaxy where no being had ever achieved this distinction and he was ready to profit from it. The Chancellor, the leader of a once powerful society, couldn't wait for Hecor to depart. All during this time the Benari fleet continued to reduce its forces and a new set of complicated laws were transmitted to everyone.

At the Benari scientific institution Dengy and Ale prepared for the first virtual entry into Ceylar's mind. The L416 processor was a tall unit requiring the user to place a featherweight hood over their head. Ale ran him through a checklist and then glanced over at Dr. Tralin. "I think we're ready to go."

"Very well."

"Ceylar's communicative interface has been initiated. I'm now adjusting the processor to match his wave cycle." Ale placed the hood on Dengy's head and then took her seat behind the control monitors. "I'm shutting you down at the first sign of trouble."

"Don't be too quick. I can pull myself out."

"I'm more concerned with our patient."

"Oh, thanks." He spoke to Dr. Tralin. "I'm going to attempt a simple intrusion to find out if we have any real communication."

Tralin and Golbot stood on each side of their friend and put there hands on his chest to enable Dengy's entrance. At first Dengy's vision went black and then an explosion of colorful forms swirled around him. At first the forms were indistinguishable, but soon changed to geometric surfaces and then into pink and orange mountains and red and green rivers. Ale carefully guided him through the brain channels best suitable to contact Ceylar. Feeling as if he were losing his balance, Dengy tried stumbling towards what resembled a large silver and blue leafless tree. He stopped short of it when noticing a strange creature with grayish brown hair, burning red pear shaped eyes and a scowling mouth full of sharp teeth. "This is really weird."

The creature, whose teeth dripped with blood, saw Dengy

and charged at him at full speed. He froze in terror and then pulled himself out of the interface.

"What happened in there?" asked Ale.

"I wasn't prepared for the chaos. I freaked."

Tralin walked over to him. 'What did you see?"

"I didn't make contact with Ceylar, if that's what you mean? And if this first foray is indicative of what's going on in his mind, it's pretty terrible. It was like a nightmare and there were some ugly things in there."

"What do you want to do?"

"Go back. Now that I know what to expect, I won't be startled. I know I can't be harmed by anything in there."

Ale activated the processor and Dengy immersed himself into Ceylar's mind. There were triangular forms filled with disjointed images of places and beings from all over the galaxy. The sky was black and then lavender and the water in the rivers changed colors erratically. The water turned into a boiling torrent of multiple headed insects and the monster he had previously seen was back. It charged at him again and opened its mouth to swallow him whole. But Dengy just ignored the assault and passed right through it. The sea of insects developed multiple wings and started flying upward. One of them flew at him with dangling claws and tried to pick him off the ground. The air around him began to swirl green and blue and the flying monsters all blended together in the sky. "This is really getting strange. If Ceylar's still with us, he's in an awful place. It's just plain scary." Just then a blubbery creature with dozens of eyeballs on the end of protruding tentacles bounced over his head.

* *

Talisa sat outside the mountaintop estate and enjoyed the rays of the afternoon sun. Though impervious to any kind of burn, she could still allow the forces of nature to interact with her without compromising her immortality. A few timid wild animals bravely crept up to her and she tossed bits of food at them. They kept their distance while birds flew overhead; one of them a large reptilian indigenous to the planet. The animals certainly prey for the beast, felt comfortable in Talisa's presence.

"Don't worry little ones. I won't let it get you."

Javensbee meandered over to her and the animals scattered. "They apparently don't like me very much."

She held out her hand and pulled him close to her. "I've made an important decision. I want to live with you."

He was delighted. "Excellent. I never thought I'd hear you say that."

"You've done a great job seducing me."

"Then this is monumental." He sensed she was apprehensive. "But there is something wrong."

"There is something wrong. If I am going to be your mate and we are going to live together, then I have a favor to ask."

"Name it."

"End this war. End the Makeo occupation."

"Done."

"That's it?"

"I never intended of handing this galaxy over to an idiot like General Hecor. He was a ploy to get your attention."

"We could have prevented all this."

"I doubt it. It was necessary. Is there anything else?"

"Yes, Javensbee. I want to lead as normal a life as possible. Is that something you're going to be able to cope with?"

"If I am to become a useful patron of this galaxy, then I must learn how to behave in what you call a normal manner. But now, I have a general to visit."

General Hecor and two of his generals sat in his private

quarters inside the lead battle cruiser. They were laughing and drinking and congratulating themselves on their great victory.

"Here's a toast to our new supreme leader. Or should I say, beloved leader?"

Hecor belched, then laughed and smashed his glass into the general's. "I like the sound of that."

"When are we going home? I'm tired of this space."

Hecor gulped down a throat full. "Today we go home triumphantly. I've been told they're arranging a big parade for us."

"We deserve it!"

Hecor leaned over and spoke softly. "There is something I want to discuss with you. You are my most trusted aides and I feel I can confide in you."

"Tell us, tell us?"

"Now that we are conquerors, there's no reason for us not to enjoy some of the benefits. We don't have to share everything with the Makeo Empire."

"What do you mean?"

"We haven't come this far just to give everything back to our citizens. We owe them prosperity and protection, but not all the wealth."

"I'm beginning to see your point."

"There are many worlds that will pay dearly for our protection, if you know what I mean?"

"Count us in."

Lieutenant Fecan interrupted on the intercom. "We're ready to depart in two hours."

"I'll be on the bridge soon."

The Makeo fleet prepared to leave Benari space. Hecor had given orders to leave four battle cruisers on permanent patrol as a show of force. He soon joined Fecan on the bridge and was met with bows from all the crew. Javensbee rode up an elevator and walked into the middle of the bridge. "Oh, it's you, Oribud. Your presence is not needed at this time."

126

"True, but I wish to have a word with you before we depart."

He was dismissive. "Yes, what is it?"

"I've decided to end our relationship."

"You've decided?" The rest of the crew silently gasped. "Did it ever occur to you that I am the one in charge here?"

"You may think you are, but you are mistaken."

"Arrogant, Oribud. That's going to lead to your death. You have served me well, but I don't need you any longer. Sooner or later you'll turn the weapon on me. It's as good a time as any to dispose of you."

"You are a fool Hecor; and a petty dictator."

"You've just insulted the supreme leader of the galaxy for the last time."

Lieutenant Fecan grabbed his sidearm weapon. "I'll kill him where he stands."

Hecor nodded confidently. "That's a fitting end to our comrade."

Fecan lifted his weapon, aimed at Javensbee's chest and shot him with the laser which absorbed into his body. Everyone just stared in disbelief.

"You'll have to do better than that."

Four other bridge officers unloaded a barrage of beams into his face and chest. "What's going on here?" Hecor asked alarmingly.

"You see, General. You never knew who you were dealing with." Javensbee formed into a white hot sphere and forced the crew to cover their eyes. The white heat spread throughout the cruiser and exploded the hull into fingernail size splinters of metal. Javensbee then darted from cruiser to cruiser and they were all eliminated in turn. With the entire fleet of cruisers destroyed, the remaining support vessels retreated hastily through the Relemark system at high speeds.

The Benarian Chancellor was sleeping in his quarters when he was awoken by an exact duplicate of himself. He sat up surprised and glanced around disorientated. "What's going on here?"

"My apologies, Chancellor. We don't have much time. You're going to thank me about this later. I'm going to give you a mild concussion." He held out his hand, blurred the air between them, and the Chancellor fell back unconscious on the bed. Javensbee exited the room and the guard stood at attention.

Another officer came running down the hallway, shouting, "Hecor's dead, Hecor's dead! There was a massive explosion. The fleet's in retreat!"

"Calm down, I know. Prepare a communication with the Makeo home world and gather my admirals."

"Yes sir, right away."

Javensbee strolled down the hallway and was met by three admirals; who were also stupified by the recent developments. They asked a succession of questions but were waved off by Javensbee. They arrived at the main conference room and Javensbee stood across from the monitor screen. A distraught Makeo general appeared. "I'm Nalosi. I'm in temporary command."

"Very well, General Nalosi. No doubt you are baffled at what has just transpired?"

"We are at a complete loss. We have suffered a great defeat."

Javensbee smiled. "You have. An awkward position for a people that had previously ruled the galaxy." Other admirals filed into the room. "We now have the ability to destroy your civilian and military at will." Puzzled, the admirals gazed at each other. "We do not wish to seek revenge."

"Then may I ask your terms?"

"The Makeo will withdraw to their former positions according to the previous treaty. We will resume military cooperation with the desire to have further disarmament talks. It is my intention that peace be restored among the Benari and Makeo."

"Those terms are very reasonable."

"And General Nalosi, just in case you have any lingering

doubts about our abilities, you have two minutes to vacate your committee room."

Nalosi paused in disbelief, stood up and ran out of the room. Javensbee struck with a bolt of lightning which left all the contents in the room a shattered mess. It was now evident to the Makeo that the Benari possessed some kind of super weapon. He then instructed the admirals to reinstate the moored Benari fleet and restore the military to its former numbers. Javensbee left the room and returned to the Chancellor's quarters, where he vanished immediately. When the Chancellor awoken, he left the room and found his staff celebrating. "What? What happened?"

"You saved us all."

"What are you talking about?"

* ** * *

Dengy had re-entered Ceylar's mind, trekking along what seemed to be an endless road next to a river bank obscured by thorny bushes. He commented to Ale how quiet it was compared to some of the recent violent formations. He could hear rippling water and catch occasional glimpses of the blue water between the bushes. He looked ahead, but the trail seemed to go on forever. Dengy then removed the virtual hood and Ale shut down the system.

"What happened?"

"You tell me? I was going nowhere."

She received the data and shook her head. "Here's the problem. You'd have been walking along there forever. Ceylar's defense mechanism. He must have sub-consciously sensed you were seeking him and rerouted you."

Tralin came over. "What happened?"

"Good, and bad news. Ceylar is using his thoughts to detour us from finding him. That means he is aware of our presence;

and that's good news. The bad news, we have to find a way to bypass him."

"Have any ideas?"

"His mind functions like most; central receptors controlling different parts. If we could isolate that receptor, trick it into believing we're in a different region, we might be able to create a false trail like he did for us."

"Do you think it will work?"

"We have no choice. We have to reach him."

Ale entered the codes. "I'll adjust the sequencers."

For the next two hours they programmed the computer to anticipate a divertive pathway in Ceylar's thoughts. They would make progress, but then fail and have to start over. Although the sophisticated calculations were able to predetermine Ceylar's sub-conscious rerouting patterns, his brain was still outmaneuvering the computer with pathways not even mapped in medical studies.

All the while Dengy and Ale were calculating, word began to slowly spread about General Hecor's demise. The shortly lived Hecorian Empire had fallen faster than it had come to power. The Chancellor, who had no idea of what had transpired, basked in the glory of the revival of his empire. Detente had replaced war and he was eager to receive emissaries. The Benarian military fleet was restored to its former strength and the Makeo government was grateful for the benevolence shown to them. Soon General Nalosi had arranged new democratic elections to restore the Makeo's civilian government.

Javensbee returned to his mountaintop estate and was greeted with a warm embrace by an appreciative Talisa Caru. She had wondered how he was going to bring back civility to the galaxy and was surprised by the immediate results. "I must say, you made this thing right in record time."

"Nothing to it. You know that I'm efficient, if nothing else. Building up empires and tearing them down is sport to me."

She sneered while surveying the living room. "Now that this is going to be our home, I think a few changes are in order."

"It's not to your standards?"

"As far as places to live, it's quite remarkable. It's just somebody else's place. I can't help thinking about the former occupant."

"What can I say; he was a casualty of war."

"I just want to redecorate. Make it our home."

"Of course. Decorate as you will."

"And we'll have to invite Tralin and Golbot for a social gathering."

He winced. "Golbot doesn't like me very much."

"He'll have to accept you just as I have. He will have to understand that my loyalty is to you now."

"I thought I never would hear you say that."

"Don't get the wrong idea. I'm not going to be your slave. As a matter of fact, there are a few things I want to talk to you about."

"Oh...?"

"I don't intend to spend eternity being a housewife."

"That wouldn't fit your personality."

"You said you wanted to contribute to the well being of the galaxy?"

"I'm prepared to help the citizens, not harm them."

"Good, because I intend to continue my work as a mercenary. And I want you to be a part of that."

"I would be most honored. But I must say that mercenary work is completely foreign to me."

"And there won't be any snapping of fingers to solve every problem. If you're going to lead a normal life, you have to play it normal."

"That I'm not so keen on."

"So was everything a lie?"

He walked away from her, carefully choosing his next words. "No, but I could make mercenary work so much easier."

"I don't want it be easier. Life is…not expecting the turnout you intended sometimes."

"All right. We'll do it your way."

"Good." She pecked him on the cheek. "I have a mission in the bad lands of Jarconi. There's this small planet under siege. They have a fairly intricate shield system, but not much else. We have to figure out how to open a supply route."

* *

Dengy had hoped it would be a matter hours before they could delve back into Ceylar's mind; but it was actually two days later. Once Ale stumbled upon a relatively inert brain pathway, they were able to reconfigure the virtual processor to stay ahead of Ceylar's thoughts. When they prepared a juncture relay to counteract the rerouting defences, Dengy put on the hood and prepared to enter.

"Everything looks good", Ale stated emphatically.

"Let's see if we can get back to the river trail."

Dengy found himself in a chaotic landscape where planets seem to spin and converge on one another behind a backdrop of bombastic rainbows. When the planets came together they morphed into gold spheres with talking mouths over the surfaces. The mouths grew larger and eventually swallowed up the spheres, which in turn split into smaller squares. "Everything seems normal so far, if you can call this normal." The rainbows swirled into flat red and silver sheets and then changed into strange insects of all varieties. The insects attacked Dengy, but he just brushed them aside unfazed and delved further into Ceylar's sub-conscious.

He came upon a desert of brown and silver sand dunes where flying creatures with hundreds of wings and non discernable heads leaped out of the ground and bumped into each other, forming much larger creatures. They kept devouring each other until there was just one giant big ball of flapping wings wallowing over the dunes. Dengy took one step forward and was taken back to the river trail with the thorny bushes. Ale compensated for the diversion and Dengy passed through the thorns and walked over the river.

"It worked. I'm through."

He pursued a path through a series of colorful landscapes and nightmarish monsters, of which he easily overcame. He stood on the shore of a large blue lake with an island in the middle with rocks haphazardly placed on top of others. He could sense that he was near to Ceylar, but could not see him. He called out, but there was no response. He stepped out onto the lake and sunk to the bottom; but was able to traverse the lake bottom with ease. In the murkiness, there were sea creatures with long necks and vicious teeth snapping at him continually. They swarmed around him and he just plowed through the waters.

Dengy stepped on the shore of the island where a thirty foot stretch of sandy beach led up to the base of the piled up rocks. The mound had huge boulders on the bottom and smaller rocks above, but didn't appear to have an entrance. "I believe I have found Dr. Ceylar. He's built some kind of fortress around him. I'm going to create a doorway of sorts in my thoughts. I don't want to unduly alarm him. I don't want to seem like an invader. I want to present myself in a conventional manner."

"Everything looks good on our end."

"I'm going in." Dengy slipped through the rock with ease until he came to the last few inches of the inner wall. His mind produced a rock door with a handle which he opened to reveal a small cavern with a disheveled bald dark skinned Benarian cowering against the back wall. Dengy slowly approached him. "It's all right. I'm a friend. My name is Dengy."

He didn't answer, just pressed harder up against the wall.

"Is your name Dr. Ceylar?"

He shook his head. "No."

"Then what is your name? I'm not going to harm you." He reached out and delicately touched Ceylar's shoulder.

"My name is Andropdi."

"Are you a geologist?"

"Yes."

"You built a really good shelter here."

Ceylar stood up. "I had to. There were so many horrible beasts out there."

"I know. I came that way. But I was able to defeat them all. I know a way of getting out of here."

He fell back against the wall. "No, it's too dangerous!

EIGHT

THE BENARI AND MAKEO HAD restored all the law and edicts of the original peace treaty. In the spirit of forgiveness and reconciliation there was a monument constructed in orbit around the Katus settlement. It was a series of pylons mounted on a rectangular base and would commemorate the tragedy that had sparked the collapse of civil discourse. Although there would never be a final determination of fault, political leaders vowed they would never go to war again.

Talisa and Javensbee were at maximum speed on their way to their first joint mission. Javensbee was understandably bored at the length of time it took to arrive there. He monitored the ship's operation and received intermittent communications as they maneuvered through several planets and orbiting space stations. Talisa was used to mundane methods of travel and was amused by her lover's dissatisfaction. They sat down on a couch in the main cabin and Talisa activated a view screen. "If all goes well, we should get there in a few days."

"I can hardly wait."

She stroked his cheek. "Oh, poor baby. Things a little slow?"

"No, I love to creep from world to world."

"Let's get down to business. There are two species in this solar system; one the Elupi, an inferior military power, and the Ubriac, the more dominant."

"So we'll be employed by the Elupi?"

"You know me well."

"How about I pay a visit to the Ubriac and end this thing real quick?" He stared at her for a moment, and then shook his head. "I didn't think so. You like doing things the the hard way."

"Here's a map of the system. As you can see the Ubriac planet is mostly barren. They have a few orbiting colonies, but they've exhausted most of their natural resources. On the other hand the Elupi planet is lush, with vegetation and rich in minerals. It's a classic dilemma."

"What is the strategic situation at the moment?"

"The Elupi have taken a defensive posture. They have a fairly advanced shielding grid that keeps them safe from attack. The Ubriac enjoy twice the numbers in military, including fighter vessels. They are warriors, always have been."

"The Elupi are prisoners in their own world and cannot get supplies. And you're going to tell me it is our task to free them."

"You catch on fast."

"I assume that Talisa Caru has a winning strategy?"

"Not exactly. I haven't had much time to study the situation while chasing down Dr. Ceylar. But I'm sure that you and I can find some solution."

"I have one already."

She smirked. "I'll bet you do. The Ubriac have been intimidating supply ships; confiscating goods. Foreign supply ships have been unwilling to challenge them."

"A classic tactic."

"It's up to us to poke holes in that tactic."

* *

Dengy and Ale worked feverishly on the calculations as Ceylar lay in a coma at the institution. Golbot was noticeably impatient, but Tralin kept everything into perspective; reminding him that any misstep could lead to irretrievable damage. The Benarian Chancellor, at the apex of his newly acquired stature, arranged a meeting with the interim representatives of the civilian Makeo government. They all assembled in the main conference room and the Chancellor called the meeting to order.

"We're here to establish protocols of governance. A permanent democratically elected Makeo government must be installed. I'm happy to introduce the temporary Makeo President, Revu, who I know is very popular with his people. I believe Revu to be the one that will lead the Makeo through a peaceful transition.

"Thank you for those inspiring words, Chancellor. Indeed it is a monumental occasion and one that has the promise that our peoples will live in peace for thousands of years. I'm pleased at this time to announce that all the Benari military sites have been returned to their rightful owners. This of course in conjunction with reestablishment of the Benari fleet."

"Thank you, Revu. And in the next six months our joint governments plan to establish several committees with expertise in military, commercial, transportation and judicial. It is imperative that we honor the edicts that have worked so well in our past."

"The Chancellor and I will be meeting on a daily basis for some time to come. We have instructed our aides to report on several fronts. This is not going to be an era of passive government involvement. On the contrary we intend to be duly vigilant in all aspects. We can never again allow the carnage that took place under General Hecor and his misguided followers. We must assure all of our citizens that subterfuge will not repeat under our rule."

"Thank you, Mr., President."

"Furthermore it is my intention to call for elections for all Makeo communities as soon as that is possible. Makeo will return to its better days."

* *

"Time to drop out of light speed."

"Finally. It couldn't come sooner.

"No doubt we'll be met by a Ubriac welcoming committee."

Javensbee's eyes twinkled. "Good, our first altercation."

"Remember, we're not looking for a fight."

"Of course not. Why would we want to prevail?" He cocked his head. "Are you sure you really are that great mercenary fighter?"

Elupi appeared in the view screen and Talisa reduced speed to five hundred miles per hour. Six Ubriac scout vessels flanked them and they were hailed. On screen a Ubriac officer, muscular with a vest and exposed arms, glared at her with a fierce countenance. "This is disputed space. You'll have to submit to a cargo inspection."

"We are not hostile."

"The Ubriac are at war with the Elupi. No contraband passes through."

Talisa gazed over at Jevensbee, and then back at the officer. "I won't allow you to search my vessel. But you're welcome to scan us."

"That's unacceptable."

"If you scan my ship you'll see I have a formidable arsenal, probably more potent than twenty of your vessels. Now if we get into a fight, we may lose. On the other hand, we might win."

The officer cut off communication and Talisa winked at Javensbee. "I know the kind. He knows I can destroy him before reinforcements arrive."

The Ubriac officer came back on screen. "Your terms are acceptable. It appears you're not carrying contraband."

"Thank you. That's what I've been telling you."

The six ships veered off to resume their patrol. Talisa contacted the Elupi, who directed them to an entry point in the shield grid. Javensbee analyzed the energy shield with Talisa's instrumentation. "It's fairly impressive. Sophisticated even for their limited technology. They've designed a series of buoys with relays to the surface. They've accounted for fluctuation weakness by alternating relays. The Ubriac are unable to penetrate such a system."

"And thus the stale mate."

They slipped under the grid and were greeted by two Elupi escort vessels that guided them to the green and blue surface. They were met by guards at the capital city and were instructed to follow them to the court where the King ruled. Unlike the Ubriac, the Elupi were reptilian beings with green body hair on their faces, arms and legs. They were taken through a series of white and gray domed structures; the prevailing architecture. The Elupi King held out his arms joyously and showed them to a table of delicacies. "We are unaware of your culinary preferences. This variety should suit you."

"Everything looks delicious. But we're not hungry now."

"Then we shall get down to business."

"This is my partner, Javensbee."

"We are honored, sir." He stretched out his claw to shake his hand."

"The pleasure is mine."

"Come this way to the arboretum. We find the plants in this room to be quite soothing for negotiations."

They entered a domed structure with dangling plants and rows of soft leaved trees. They sat at a wooden table where Talisa folded her hands on top. "Payment can be discussed later. The Elupi integrity precedes you."

"We are honored by your compliments."

"So why the hostilities?" asked Javensbee.

The King swigged liqueur from a mug. "Our two races weren't always like this; at war. Centuries ago we had good relations with the Ubriac. And then their natural resources began to dwindle. At that time our leaders had the foresight to start construction on our energy shield. Ten years ago the Ubriac demanded parcels of our land for mineral development. We offered to share, but we refused to give them land. That is when they initiated the blockade. Up until recently, we were able to get supplies. But they have become more efficient with their blockade."

"So they intend to take your land one way or the other. Typical siege mentality. But effective."

"You are correct, Javensbee."

Talisa tapped her chin. "If I'm correct, their forces outnumber you three to one?"

"Unfortunately you are correct. We are no match for their military."

"Then we'll have to draw them to us."

The King nodded. "We tried that and were unsuccessful. We disabled one of our buoys, hoping they would come through the grid. They didn't attack."

Javensbee sneered. 'Of course they didn't. They saw it for what it was."

"What choice did we have?"

"Please understand I didn't mean offense. It's not a bad strategy. It just needs to be done right. I've observed your grid system and I compliment you on its sophistication. I've seen these types of protective shields before and the use of alternating frequencies. But these kinds of shields always have a weakness that you or your enemy may not know about."

"Are you saying we have such a weakness?"

Talisa smiled. "You can trust that if my partner says there's a weakness, there's a weakness."

"It's an odd quirk of physics. I'd like to go up and investigate it more thoroughly. If I can isolate the weakest area, then we just may be able to deceive your enemy into believing there's a way in."

"It's difficult for me to accept such a weakness, but you are the experts."

Talisa and Javensbee maneuvered her ship into an orbital pattern just underneath the shield's protection. While a few

Ubriac vessels patrolled above them, they took readings on the shield modulations.

"What makes you so sure there is this weakness?"

"Even your instruments are unable to detect it. No offense.

"None taken."

"If you'd allow me to shed this prison of yours, I could give you a quick answer."

"No, let's do it the normal way."

"Right. A planet's magnetic fields play havoc with these kinds of grids. They could manifest anywhere, but often stabilize in one place for years."

After three hours surveying the grid, Javensbee ordered her to stop. "I found it. In sector 5.761G according to Elupi coordinates."

"You can sense it?"

"No, your instruments are detecting it. But I could have found it sooner."

She was stunned. "There it is. A short burst from a Ubriac vessel and it would knock a small hole until the buoys could compensate."

"This is where we set our trap."

"What did you have in mind?"

* *

Dengy and Ale had completed their calculations and were ready to proceed with the final operation. Unlike their repairs of the communication neurons, this procedure would require thousands of more intricate fusion links. The method of heating and sealing off strands would be similar, but now mistakes could permanently damage the higher brain functions. Dr. Tralin was anxious to get started, but Dengy was more cautious, re-examining his calculations before proceeding. They began the operation in the early part of the evening.

Perspiration beaded across Dengy's face as his hand unsteadily quivered at every stage of the repairs. Ale was much calmer and toiled effortlessly on her task. Dr. Tralin and Golbot kept their hands over Dr. Ceylar, who was oblivious to the procedure. Twelve grueling hours later, and without fanfare or a congratulatory speech, Dengy shut off the machinery. "It's done."

Exhausted, Ale's forehead fell against her control panel. "Everything here seems to indicate complete success."

Tralin walked over to Dengy. "Brilliant. So what is next?"

"I've got to take a break, and then we can go back inside and see if Dr. Ceylar's health is back to normal."

Pregnant and exhausted, Ale appreciated the time to clean up and take a short nap. A couple hours later they were back at the control units. Dengy placed the hood visor over his head and prepared to enter Ceylar's thoughts. Once Ale programmed the instrumentation, Dengy emerged into the formally chaotic regions of Ceylar's mind. The monsters were gone, along with the wild moving colors and swirling geometric figures. Dengy was in a soundless landscape of airy whiteness. "Initially, I'd say we've been successful. I'm going to bring myself to the lake and the rock island."

Dengy concentrated on the place he knew Ceylar was hiding and it appeared before him. He stepped up to the edge the waters and flew over the surface, free from any attacking creatures. He came to the rocky mound, created the interior door to Ceylar's cave and found Dr. Ceylar meticulously groomed with a trimmed beard and well pressed clothes. He smiled at Dengy and then embraced him. "You came back for me!"

"I told you I would, Andropodi. It is Andropodi?"

"Yes, it's me? You told me you would come back and you did."

"You look well."

"I haven't felt this wonderful in so many years. I'm not afraid."

"Excellent. I knew you would recover. And now I'd like to

take you back to your college study. You would like to go there, right?"

He excitedly leaped in the air. "Yes, my old study!"

Dengy pointed to the rock door. "It's just on the other side of that door."

He reverted to skepticism. "Really? It doesn't seem possible."

"You trust me, don't you?"

He grinned warmly. "Yes. Dengy, you saved my life."

"I'll go first."

He opened the door wide and Ceylar followed right behind him. They stood in Ceylar's college campus study, an old fashioned room with a hearth, fireplace, thick wooded furniture and spongy leather chairs. There were computers and modern technology; but as Dengy had stated to all of them, Dr. Ceylar would fill in the details from memories stored in Andropodi's mind. Still, Dengy was relieved that the operation had not degraded Ceylar's recollection prior to being a geologist.

Dr. Ceylar touched and caressed the items in the room that were so dear to him. He thanked his new friend for restoring his sanity. He swore to Dengy that he would remain safely in the study until told differently. He reclined in one of the soft chairs and closed his eyes, sniffing the leathery odors. "I have to go for a short time, Andropodi. But I will return."

"I'll be fine here. I am at home. This is where I belong."

"Do you mind if I ask you a few questions? They may seem odd."

"Go ahead."

"How long have you been a geologist?"

"Twenty years, now. Teaching for five."

"And you have never heard of the Mist?"

"No. Should I?"

"No. And you've never heard of Javensbee?"

"I know nothing of Javensbee?"

"I thought you may have heard about them. But not to worry. I'll be going"

Dr. Ceylar stretched his arms over his head and yawned. "I think I should like to rest for a while. It has been a trying ordeal."

"That's a good idea." Dengy walked out of the study door, pulled his visor off and wandered over to Ceylar's resting body. "Medically, I have cured this patient. We have a new technique to cure many of these kinds of diseases. But it has failed to bring Dr. Ceylar back to his former self."

"But he is cognoscente. We have hope."

"We do have hope. The next faze is to get into his memory. See if we can restore it to its full capacity."

"How much damage do you think there is?"

"That's the unknown. Science has practically mapped everything about memory and how we respond to it. The only problem is; we really don't know how it works."

"Should we consider bringing him out of the coma? Is that even possible?"

"Dr. Tralin, I'm not sure about anything. Technically, we should be able to bring him out of the coma. There's nothing really wrong with that part of his brain. But I'd be hesitant to do that at this time. The shock could send him further into regression. We could lose him forever; and that's horrifying for an eternal being."

"Then we'll leave the decision to you."

* *

Javensbee huddled around the Elupi King and his military officers, studying a view screen of the planet's shield grid. "Talisa and I have located the weakness in you system. The Ubriac were unable to scan it because they weren't close enough and were not looking for it. As you can see, the weakness is there while all the buoys are functioning properly. They have been trying to deactivate the buoys and you were trying to trick them into believing could."

"So you have a plan?"

He winked at Talisa. "We do. Nonetheless, you and your people will have to think about increasing your military numbers. Your days of passive defensive methods are over. For now, we have to even out the playing field. I'm going to pilot one of your vessels with a full cargo of minerals. Talisa will be following in her ship. The Ubriac have already scanned her ship and will send a large contingency to overwhelm the weapon's superiority. We'll make a run for the weak spot and my vessel will be destroyed on impact with the grid. Talisa will escape, and the pursuing vessels will find the anomaly when at close range. They may be clever enough to escape an obvious trap, but this one will appear with a fully operational grid."

The King was apprehensive. "So they will send their ships into our air space? We would be allowing an invasion."

"Yes", Talisa interrupted. "We figure a hundred ships could make it in before we close the rift and misdirect the anomaly."

"Won't they see our vessels waiting for them?"

"That's where I come in. I have clocking technology that will render us invisible. We can derive power off the neighboring buoys. They won't detect us until they're well inside the grid."

"It seems risky."

"You have no real choice here. Face it your Excellency, your options are not that good. This way you can commandeer vessels and hostages."

"My partner's right. It's the only way."

"Then we shall do as you say."

Talisa caru toiled for hours adjusting the parameters of the energy buoys to interact with her clocking devices. Javensbee's vessel was equipped with a cargo of minerals and was given instructions on how to operate it. Talisa boarded her ship and communicated with her partner. "All systems at peek efficiency."

145

"I have a little wager, my love. You interested?"

"What do have in mind?"

"We're timing this thing close. I'm betting you will not be able to beam me over before my ship is destroyed."

"I think I can with seconds to spare."

"Then it's a bet? If I was mortal, I'd be your dead partner."

"What's the stakes?"

"If I win, I get to sit in on the Ubriac high command military meeting when they find about the anomaly."

"And if I win, I want to give that property back to the rightful owner's family."

"Reasonable."

Both ships left the protection of the grid and flew towards Ubriac space. Soon a patrol of sixty vessels approached them at high speeds and scanned their vessels. When the attack began, Javensbee positioned his vessel directly behind Talisa's as it took the brunt of the lasers and missiles. She returned fire and then steered back towards Elupi with Javensbee now in front of her. The Ubriac vessels barraged the shields of both ships, damaging Javensbee's shields much more than hers. Talisa protected him as much as possible, but her ship was being fired upon from all directions.

The grid was in view when Talisa pulled slightly ahead of Javensbee, allowing his vessel to be more vulnerable. Just miles before impact, Javensbee's vessel was struck with a deadly torpedo and smashed into the grid and disintegrated; allowing Talisa's ship to pass through undamaged. The Ubriac fleet pulled up at the last second, but not until they discovered the anomaly.

Javensbee materialized in the cockpit, gloating with a brash grin. "Well, well. Looks like I was killed."

"I was a micro second from snatching you."

"How seconds can seem like an eternity."

"Okay, Javensbee. You won."

He snapped his fingers and vanished. Talisa returned to the Elupi command and prepared the clocking devise and the Elupi vessels for ambush. Javensbee wiggled and rippled through the walls and corridors of the Ubriac military headquarters where the leaders were about to receive the report. The lead pilot entered the room where his superiors discussed their strategy.

"The report, sir. We were able to destroy the Elupi cargo vessel. The foreigner's vessel escaped into the grid."

"How unfortunate. We have learned that your adversary was a soldier for hire named Talisa Caru. It would have been to your credit had she been destroyed."

"My apologies, sir. But we did receive some valuable information."

"What's that?"

"We detected a strange interruption in the grid when the Elupi vessel collided with it. It appears to be a deficiency in the grid itself. The buoys were all working properly."

"Why did we not find it previously?"

"Our close proximity made it possible."

"Are you certain of this?"

"Our scientists have verified it."

He slammed his fist on the table jubilantly. "That's it! We have a way in. Assemble a fleet of two hundred vessels. Let's take this planet."

"You'll have battle plans within an hour, sir."

Javensbee re-materialized in the cockpit of Talisa's ship. "They have taken the bait and they'll be on their way shortly."

"How many?"

"Two hundred. We should close the grid at one hundred or so. That seems like a manageable number for us."

"I agree."

"The vessels should be cloaked immediately."

The Elupi command detected the Ubriac fleet on course directly towards the weakened grid area. The invisible Elupi vessels flanked each side of the entry point and waited for orders to attack. Talisa positioned her ship in such a way to fall behind the Ubriac and chase any vessels that elude the main force. As expected the Ubriac ships began to fire upon the weakened area and opened a fissure; penetrating the grid one by one. Feeling confident of victory, they did not detect the Elupi until it was too late. A sudden barrage of weapons from each side rendered at least one hundred and twenty vessels inoperative. After the Elupi reinforced the grid, the remaining Ubriac vessels abandoned the raid and fled back to their space. The captured vessels were boarded and the crews transferred to a heavily guarded holding facility. The vessels were then flown to a military base where they would be put into service by the Elupi. The commandeered vessels would not bring parody with the Ubriac forces, but would significantly degrade their abilities to maintain a full quarantine.

The Ubriac leader contacted the Elupi King. He was angry, upset and pompous, but his threats were now tempered. "This has been an outrageous theft."

"Forgive me for the deception, but you left me no choice."

"What are your intentions?"

"We will reinforce our cargo routes. But it is my hope and desire that we can come to some kind of detente; perhaps even becoming trading partners. It would be in both our interests to avoid war."

"Your offer has merit. I will discuss it with my people."

"Tomorrow we will send out a convoy of supply ships. It is our hope that the Ubriac will not attack."

"We will not interfere."

Talisa and Javensbee remained at Elupi to celebrate the victory. Although they were paid what Javensbee had considered a paltry sum, he accepted her reasons for such generosity. They headed back to their mountaintop estate and reclined in the cabin through the quietness of space. "Javensbee, I have to admit that you performed excellently."

He leaned back proudly. "Using basic skills to help out an inferior species has its rewards."

"There's hope for you yet."

"I still say it was a lot of trouble for very little payment."

"And I've learned that you're quite the tactician when it comes to military skills. This was all your idea and it worked very well."

"Helping out a bunch of lizards is child's play compared to my recent manipulation of the entire galaxy. But I'll take that as a compliment."

"You and I make a great team."

"Talisa, we will be that for an eternity."

* *

Dengy and Ale carefully studied the best method of interacting with Ceylar's memory. They had repaired all the brain damage and access to the memory center should be simple in comparison. The main problem was that the L416 virtual processor was not visually adaptable with the memory regions of the brain. Ale stared at her husband with a blank expression. "We're not dealing with the biological, but the metaphysical."

"Accessing is easy, but entering the memory itself may not be possible."

"Agreed. Memory to Ceylar is passive. Something he can think about."

"The sub-conscious is an active receptor, only hidden. And memory is still biological, only inactive. We can read thoughts, but only the patient can relay them to us. We have to find out a way to get inside and see what's going on."

"Maybe an inactive approach could do it? We have to reconfigure our equipment and not try to understand how Dr. Ceylar's complexities."

Dengy's eyes bulged. "That's it! Let's bring some light."

"What do you mean?"

"A KX05 processor."

"A spectral analyzer?"

"Yeah…a KXO5. It's primitive compared to the L416, but we can use it to assimilate the data from the L416 provides."

"You're right, Dengy. A processor to read the processor. A translator. Could it be that simple?"

Dengy nodded at Tralin. 'We can use light to paint a picture. I know we have several devices in stock."

The KX05 unit was much smaller than the more elaborate processor. Although incompatible, they could program a modulator realignment used by other scientists to connect diametrically opposed machinery. Soon Dengy and Ale had reconfigured both units and were prepared for the first excursion into Ceylar's memory.

"Dr. Tralin, there are a few things I must explain. Memory restoration, that is the loss of memory due to senility or disease has been successful for centuries. But in all those circumstances, it was done in direct communication with the patient. We do not have that advantage because we can not allow Ceylar knowledge of our task."

"Whether it works or not, we have no choice but to try."

Dengy placed the hood visor over his head and Ale initiated the sequence. "I'm going to report what I see. Hopefully I will see something. I'm entering memory now and I have visual. The processor is working. It appears I'm in a large room, tall, tall ceiling; whitish beige walls. This is really strange. It's full of people, all sorts. They're sitting in chairs waiting for something. They're all holding papers with numbers written on them. There's a big board overhead with numbers flashing. I see Dr. Ceylar waiting in a chair. I'm going over to him. I'm asking him where we are, but he doesn't seem to know I'm here. Bizarre. He doesn't seem to have awareness in memory. He's looking at me, just not responding. People keep getting up when their numbers are called. Must be some memory of his. And one other thing. Ceylar's appearance is like he is today. It's not like he's younger. He's talking; saying that he has to go. I'm following him out of the room. We're now in a completely different realm. We're on a city road of some kind. There's concrete everywhere. I see tall skyscrapers. This is a major city of some kind. The walls of the buildings are starting to crack. They're cracking and chipping away. They seem to be floating down to the ground; not in big chunks. But like rain. Here come some big square boulders towards us on the road. Ceylar's trying to walk to the side of road to avoid them, but they keep coming. This boulder is pinning us against the wall, we can't move. Wait, now we're walking again. More boulders are sliding towards us. We can't seem to get out of the way. Ceylar's complaining about them. He says we have to go; and now we're somewhere else. In a café of some kind. But we're still in a city. What kind of experiences are these? I can't determine that if I can't communicate with him. This is not what I expected. It should be his memories, childhood, young adult; things of that nature. But nothing makes sense. Now we're gone; in another building. There's a staircase with these people in uniform climbing up them. They have sticks, clubs, I guess. They're thumping them in their hands. They're telling us to come along. Ceylar doesn't want to go. Now we're in a forest; a beautiful green forest. There's a mountain range in the distance, and what the hell is that! There's a huge wave of water, it must be a thousand feet high, sitting on top of the mountains. It's not moving; just set in place. Now he wants to go and we're in some carnival. There are these acrobats. One of them is grabbing the arm of another and swinging them around. The arm came off. The acrobats are eating each other. You've got to be kidding me. This stuff couldn't have happened. Now we're in space, traveling in this invisible ship. We're all in chairs with planets flying by. This is more like a dream than a memory center. Okay, we're walking through a swamp. It's quiet, dripping water everywhere. Ceylar is sinking into the mud and doesn't seem interested. A boat just came by and we're on it with dry clothes. Lovely ladies are serving food. We're not getting anywhere with this. I need to know if there are any real memories to retrieve. This is not what I expected. I'm coming out."

Dengy lifted the visor off and Ale turned off the processor.

"What happened in there? All systems we're functioning normally."

"I don't know. Run a side by side comparison with the brain patterns of the visuals we just received. See what we got."

They're both the same. Exact."

Tralin walked over to him. "What does that mean?"

"I'm not sure. But do me a favor, Dr. Tralin. Let me access your memory?"

Dengy connected Dr. Tralin and Ale ran the program. "Okay I'm in. Yes, it's just like before. We're in a store. Some weird stuff; shut it off..."

"That's what I was thinking. What does this all mean, Dengy?"

"Memory, at least memory how we think of it, does not manifest like a computer would store it. You thought about that store and accessed it."

"Yes, I remember it very clearly.

"But to me, your past was just a jumbled patchwork of visuals. I knew you were in a store, but it was vague. And in Dr. Ceylar's memory center, those things may have made sense to him; who knows?"

"I don't follow you."

"I'm going to contact Ceylar again in his study; try one more thing." He placed the visor on his head and opened the door to Ceylar's study, where Dr. Ceylar warmly greeted him. "How are you, Andropodi?"

"I'm just fine, Dengy. Good to see you again."

"Would you do me a favor? Think about some childhood memory. Something you have a fond memory of."

"Certainly. My aunt's summer house. She was so wonderful to me. The trees and hills I use to play in. It was a marvelous time."

"And now can you remember what Javensbee was? Please indulge me; think?"

Ceylar just stared.

"Thank you, I'll be right back." Dengy left the study. "It's all too clear to me now. I saw a muddled interpretation of Ceylar's childhood memory much like yours, Dr. Tralin. But when I asked him to think about Javensbee, there was no response. It didn't happen to him as far as he is concerned."

"Are you saying we may not have success retrieving his memory?"

"I'm not sure there's even a memory to retrieve. What I've learned so far is that memory is real and distinctly arranged in one's own mind. But the memory center itself is really confusion, unable to relate to any mind probe with any degree of clarity. When one thinks about a memory, it's there. When one doesn't have that memory any longer, it simply cannot be manifested. And that's what we may be up against. When I asked him to remember about his childhood, it was clear as could be. But anything after his life as a geologist, there's nothing there. The biological damage he received from the disease has damaged his memory; perhaps obliterated it. You can't bring back something that's not there anymore. And as far as the memories I did see, the rocks on the road, the city; all those are themes of his geological past. But oddly enough, some of those visions were familiar to me. I can't explain it. And now we may have no option but to bring him out of the coma and explain to him that he's part of the Mist. It could be disastrous, but I fear there are no memories to retrieve."

Dr. Tralin's eyes sunk deep in his head. "This is the worst possible outcome."

"We still have a chance if we bring him out."

"You don't understand something about the Mist. It is not just a biological function that can be turned on and off like a machine. It's not a natural function like the flow of blood through the body. The Mist works very much like faith. Those beings taught us how to use the Mist; that's the best way I can describe it."

"I don't understand."

"If Ceylar does not believe he has the power, he can not just conjure the Mist as one picks up a tool to fix something. We have allowed you access to him because we have become part of him. Perhaps you're right and there is no other choice. We still may be able to teach him the ways of the Mist. But I have my doubts, Dengy. And if Ceylar can not become the Mist, then we may have to live in slavery with the Songster for the rest of eternity."

NINE

TALISA AND JAVENSBEE SPED TOWARDS a planetary system in the outer regions of the Galcon territories. They had just finished their first assignment and were hired immediately for a second. Javensbee was beginning to adjust to average methods of transportation and showed more patience as the hours of endless stars streaked past them. They relaxed in the cabin after enjoying the kind of pleasure that Talisa was craving more often.

"Tell me about this job?"

"It's a little unusual, but I've had ones like this before. We're rescuing an individual, not a planet."

"A prisoner?"

"Probably. The one hiring us is a wealthy entrepreneur name Sulifanri. His daughter, Suliganti is being held hostage."

"If he's wealthy, why not hire an army?"

"He doesn't want her harmed, or killed."

"Then we shall rescue this woman and return her to her father."

"That's the idea."

They dropped out of light speed and merged into a system where a row of multi-colored planets orbited a pulsar star. They received clearance to land on the fifth planet, a green and blue pastoral sphere. They set the ship down near a private castle in the middle of a well populated city where they followed guards through the gardens and into the main house.

A Galconian nobleman met them. "My name is Sulifanri."

"Talisa caru. This is my partner, Javensbee."

"A mutual friend has highly recommended you."

"So what has happened?"

"Please come into my parlor and make yourselves comfortable. I have this competitor in a nearby system. He does not have the power or wealth I've accumulated, but he does have certain credibility. He also has a son named Lorin. And it is he that has abducted my daughter. Our governments have suggested that we find a mutual settlement to avoid any kind of war. If you will view the monitor over there I will show you the last known confirmation of my daughter's condition."

The screen portrayed a young lady barely clothed in chains and shackles with bruises on her arms and legs. Lorin then appeared with arms crossed in defiance.

Javensbee winced. "She's not being treated kindly."

"There is one more thing you should know about my daughter. She has had prior relations with Lorin. But I do not believe she still feels the same way."

"Normally I don't take these kinds of jobs, but I owe our mutual friend. We will rescue your daughter."

"It will be difficult. She's being held in a well fortified complex in a most inhospitable jungle. It has a class 9 security shield."

"We can overcome that."

"My guards will show you to your rooms. I have taken the initiative to prepare a lavish feast for this evening."

"We are honored."

They fell in closely behind the guards and Javensbee leaned into Talisa. "What is a class 9 shield?"

"You remember the Elupi grid? It's much more formidable."

156

"Impressive"

"Don't worry; I have ways to deal with it."

After a meal and entertainment with music and dancers, Talisa cuddled up to Javensbee in their spacious bedroom suite. Morning came soon enough and they boarded the ship to review their rescue plans. She activated the main monitor. "This should be easy, I think…"

"You don't inspire confidence."

"We'll beam out at a high orbit about ten miles from the compound. We'll be just one ship of thousands visiting this planet. It's a walk through the jungle for about five miles before we encounter any real security."

"A ten mile walk. How pleasant."

"We can float the equipment until the last mile. Then we'll have to carry it to avoid detection. I've received intelligence that Lorin runs two security drills; one at day, one at night. When that happens, we'll make our move. They'll be too busy monitoring the drills."

Talisa set the coordinates and left the planet's atmosphere on route to the second planet with three tiny moons. They relayed credentials identifying themselves as Galconian traders and settled in a designated orbit. They beamed down to the landing site and materialized inside a thick blanket of humidity surrounded by large leafed plants. Talisa used a hand held device to guide a small hovering sled packed with their equipment. They fired laser pistols at the brush ahead to clear a path.

"This is what I've always wanted to do."

"It could be worse. You could be experiencing the bug bites."

Five miles into the trek she lowered the sled to the ground and removed a tubular piece of equipment. "This will neutralize any hidden sensor equipment out here."

"I know what this primitive device does."

She smiled and triggered the sled to float it through the jungle. While animal noises echoed through the trees, Javensbee misdirected the sensors when alerted to a hidden device. A large rodent with sharp teeth pounced upon him, but was instantly dispersed with a concussive arm wave. The humidity draped her clothes, but Javenbsee always remained dry.

Talisa halted their advance about a mile away from the compound, lowered the sled and removed the equipment. They carried two bags for the remainder of the hike until the jungle brush thinned and they reached the energy shield. They stood at the edge of the jungle's perimeter and waited a few hours for the sun to set and the night drill to begin. Once the grayness turned to black, they crept on their stomachs towards the class 9 shield.

"How do you propose to gain entry?"

"I purchased this little item a couple of hundred years ago from this brilliant scientist. You remember him? Domin Rysla. You killed him."

"Yes, I remember. But you could hardly blame me. He interfered."

"He tried to stop a monster. He was no threat to you."

"The past is the past, Talisa. I cannot regret what I cannot feel."

"Then, here's to Rysla. He's getting us inside this place."

"So what does this contraption do?"

"It disrupts the frequency and sends out false readings. It'll give us a few seconds to get through. We should have no problems while the drill is on." She spread the rest of the equipment out on the ground. ""We have rope, pitons and grapplers. Most importantly, these anti-gravity thrusters for repelling. I don't mind climbing, but the little princess may have difficulty."

"What about the rest of this stuff?"

"Leave it."

Talisa scanned the frequency, locked on to the signature and placed the device twenty feet away from the shield perimeter. Two short bursts carved a hole in the shield, allowing them passage without setting off any alarms. Timed precisely, it shut off as they entered the grounds.

"It's never easy with you, is it?"

She smiled. "Let's go."

They treaded through waist high plants and shrubs, eventually reaching the base of a small cliff. She removed the pitons and power shot them into the rock and then threw the grappling hooks up to the top. Securing the line, she climbed skillfully up the side of the cliff; Javensbee in tow pretending to use the equipment. At the top there was another short plateau and then a higher cliff with guard towers placed in several locations.

"They have lights."

"Time the sweep. Avoid detection."

"I could stun the guards."

"Just stick to the plan."

Lowering heads on their dash to the base of the cliff, they repeated the climb up to the next plateau. She slipped at the top where the moss was thicker, but regained her footing without being detected. Javensbee faked his exertion and joined her at the top even as a tower light strafed them. They ran up to the perimeter wall of the compound with their backs against the stone surface.

"Another climb?"

"No, there's a guard access door just around the corner. The shift change should end in a few minutes."

"You've done your research."

Talisa scanned the other side of the door for guard activity. 'Let's go." She used another scrambling device to gain entry to a courtyard and where they stealthily avoided contact with security until reaching a water fountain against a leaf covered wall. "I got it. She's being held on the third floor. My map shows a kitchen nearby. We should be able to gain access there."

* *

Dengy and Ale were analyzing thousands of calculations in order to advance their knowledge of Dr. Ceylar's memory. Frustrated, red-eyed and gloomy, they double and triple checked each variable that lead to the same daunting conclusion. No matter what they tried it ended up in failure. Ceylar's brain was essentially repaired, but his past memories didn't seem to exist. Ale tried to get her husband to accept the bleak facts, but he kept going over the results redundantly.

Finally Dr. Tralin came over and placed his hand on Dengy's shoulder. "No luck?"

"No matter what I try, it's futile."

"Then perhaps it's time to accept reality?"

He stared with bloodshot eyes. "I can't do that. We've come so far and we just can't give up."

"You said that his memory may not exist. I've been around a long time and there are some things we can never accomplish."

"So much that depends on our success. I can't quit now."

"The galaxy will have to learn to coexist with Javensbee. Perhaps we should just bring Ceylar out of his coma and take our chances."

"The shock could send him inward forever."

"Who's to say that isn't a more benevolent end?"

"Just let me go over this data a few more times. Maybe I'm missing something."

"Stop, Dengy. Go home. Get some rest."

"But Dr. Ceylar…?"

"If he could, he would tell you the same."

"I don't want to give up."

"Tell you what. Go home with your wife and get some sleep. Think about, something may come to you. And if it doesn't, we'll go on from there."

Ale put her arms around him and coaxed him out of the chair.

* *

Talisa and Javensbee gained entry into the kitchen where a few chefs applied their trade. They ducked behind the counters and easily made it into the main house. There were guards, but they were able to silently avoid them. Talisa scanned for Suliganti and found her in the same location as before. They came upon one guard standing directly in front of an elevator. Talisa whispered to Javensbee. "Do you think you could sneak up on him?"

"Even without my powers."

"Don't be smartass."

He edged along the wall and hid behind furniture. He waited, and then surprised the guard with a hand chop across his neck. They rode up the elevator to the third floor and found the hallway guard free. The readings showed Suliganti was in the room at the end, which was obviously the master bedroom. They busted into the door and Lorin and Suliganti were in the rapture of lovemaking. Two pistols were aimed at Lorin, who sprung up in bed with eyes wide open.

"Don't make a sound or you'll be killed."

Lorin became indignant. "And just who are you?"

"We're here to take your lady friend."

"My father", she huffed. "I knew he'd do something stupid."

"He wants you home."

"Tell him to drop dead!"

Talisa walked over to her. "You were in shackles."

"Of course I was. I had betrayed Lorin once before and he punished me. I deserved it. His beating was not as severe as my father's ever was."

"You're going with us, like it or not."

Confused, Javensbee leaned over and whispered. "Am I missing something here? She doesn't want to leave her lover. End of story."

"You don't quite understand this kind of work. Once I accept a job, I go through with it. Her father is a respected citizen." She smiled. "Now do me a favor and dispense with Lorin your way. But please be gentle."

"As you wish." With the flick of his hand, Lorin was knocked unconscious. Suliganti was about to scream for the guards when Talisa stunned her with a pistol. "Let's get her out this window." She removed a belt device from her bag. "Put the anti-grav around her, I'll toss out the ropes."

They repelled down the side of the building and Talisa guided Suliganti to the ground. She retrieved the gear and they ran towards the outer wall of the compound with Suliganti floating behind. A guard finally spotted them, but Javensbee quickly knocked him out from afar. They reached the access door and stopped at the edge of the larger cliff. They lowered their hostage to the ground and followed on ropes.

They remained undetected while they scaled down the side of the smaller cliff and arrived at the class 9 shield perimeter. The jamming device was undisturbed on the other side and then Talisa removed a device that reactivated the unit. They leaped through the small opening and ran towards the thick of the jungle with Suliganti close behind. One mile in they found the hover sled and began to load up all the equipment.

Suliganti opened her eyes and instantly shouted obscenities at them.

Talisa threw a spray bottle at her. "You'd better apply this quick. These insects will eat you alive."

She rubbed it into her skin, all the while cussing at them. "How could you do this to me? I will pay double my father's price."

"Look princess, what's between you and your father is your business. I was just hired to do a job. Let's get moving."

Javensbee cleared a path in the brush with a laser pistol and Suliganti kept ranting on about the heat, the bugs, her father and the humidity. Soon the clouds were so heavy that pouring rain slapped their faces. The only good thing for Suliganti was that the insects stop biting; although the rain didn't silence her raving accusations. "You just don't understand", she cried. "I love Lorin. You're ruining everything."

Disgusted, Javensbee turned around. "Will you just shut up? You haven't stopped complaining the whole time."

"You shut up. You're not the one losing your lover."

There were only two miles of trudging left, but Suliganti reminded them of her misery every inch of the way. She rambled on and on until they reached the transporter coordinates where they beamed up to the ship and immediately departed at high speeds. "There's a shower in back. Use it."

"I demand you return me!"

"I can't do that, princess. But let me give you a little advice. One day Lorin may decide you are too much of a pain in the ass to keep around."

"How dare you."

Javensbee nudged her to the back of the ship. "Just clean yourself up. Your stink is bothering me."

She stomped towards the shower and Javensbee joined Talisa in the cockpit. "I have much to learn about these species."

"She's a real winner, ehh?"

"Normally I'd just eliminate her."

Talisa grinned. "I wonder why her father even wants her back."

"She's not as beautiful as you, my dear."

"And hopefully not as much of a bitch."

"I wouldn't go that far."

Sulifanri's planet loomed in the distance. As soon as they landed on his estate, Suliganti hurried over to her father and confronted him angrily. Talisa and Javensbee followed casually and watched her jump up and down. Her father responded calmly and ordered his guards to take her into the house. He smiled at Talisa. "I appreciate your efficiency. We shall discuss a bonus." He nodded at Javensbee. "You're probably wondering why I wanted her back."

"The thought did enter my mind."

"She is my only offspring. I had always hoped that she

would take over the family business. Now I may have to include Lorin."

"She does seem headstrong."

"I thought I could plea with her one more time before giving in."

"She said that you beat her."

He laughed. "I haven't laid a hand on my daughter since she was young. It's Lorin who is the abuser."

Talisa interjected. "We're not here to pass judgment."

"I knew she wanted him, but I had to try."

* *

Ale lay quietly in the bed next to Dengy, listened to his agitated dreams and deflected his swinging arms and legs. She threw off the covers and saw that it was three o' clock in the morning. Concerned with her husband's despondency in failing to reach Ceylar, she went into the kitchen and made a cup of hot tea. She rubbed the side of the cup and stared blankly.

Dengy was still in a restless sleep when he leaped up suddenly into a seated position. "That's it!"

Startled, Ale returned to the bedroom. 'What's going on?"

He held out his arms and shouted gleefully. "It's so simple."

"What? What's so simple?"

"Sit down, sit down. Do you remember when I said there was something familiar with Ceylar's memories?

"Yes."

"I've been looking at this thing the wrong way. I've been treating the brain like a computer and it really isn't; oh there are similarities. Anyway I didn't understand why I couldn't see Ceylar's memory like I saw his consciousness in the cave. I was mostly shut out of that function, because the brain is a both a metaphysical and biological processing center. It's all thought, but thought is subjective to the individual. Ceylar still thinks he's living in real time since he met me. But his recollection

164

was something he didn't share with me; or was unable to share with me. Regardless, I couldn't make contact the way I wanted because I didn't understand the duel complexity."

This is all very interesting, but I don't see a point here when it comes to retrieving his memory."

"Memory is still there if one suffers amnesia; and you might get it back. But if the memory's not there, you can't bring back what isn't there. The disease took that away from Ceylar and it's gone forever. I know that now."

"You said that his memories were familiar?"

"That room where all the people were waiting for numbers to be called. That was my memory; or least a strange kind of melding of memories with Ceylar. When I was younger my father took me to a place that offered space excursions of all kinds. It was a bunch of different vessels taking families to worlds to explore. I remember it was a big room and depending on what number was called, that's the trip you took. And that big wave sitting on top of the mountain? You remember seeing the only known footage of the famous tsunami at Cici 5?"

"Of course, it was eight hundred feet high."

"I saw it for the first time when I was a kid. It killed millions. I was horrified. I had nightmares for years, wouldn't even go to the ocean. I still think about it. And those uniformed officers climbing the stairs slapping their batons? When I was in school, that very thing happened. They raided this place next to the school. I remember those very uniforms. They were my memories, not Ceylar's."

"I think I understand."

"Now the sliding rocks, the road, the buildings falling, those are all Ceylar's memories in some form or another. So apparently I can be part of Ceylar's memory center, as well as his sub-conscious. In simple terms, all thought is really the same. Perception may be different and the brain may have many different regions to control it; but all thought is exactly the same. It's all function."

"So how does all this help us?"

He stood on the side of the bed and smiled confidently. "Because Dr. Ceylar trusts me. And that is all we may need."

* ** *

All seemed quiet in the galaxy with life returning to the civilized days prior to General Hecor's coup. The Makeo Empire had rebuilt its government and the new president had been formally elected. There were still territories that were unmanageable, if not hostile; but there was great hope that even these places would be tamed.

Javensbee and Talisa were back at their estate preparing for a visit from Dr. Tralin and Golbot. This would be the first gathering of the Songster and the Mist in a social venue. Javensbee appeared nervous; something clearly out of character for him. He genuinely wished to repair the centuries of hatred and mistrust. He had even arranged for a circus act to perform for his guests.

"You're looking forward to this evening."

"I want to make a good impression on your friends. I do not believe they have fully accepted my transformation."

She brushed her hand across his cheek. "You can't blame them. We all have quite a history."

"Yes, a history that needs rewriting."

"They don't know you like I do. They'll come around. Tralin's a realist and he can see where this is going. On the other hand, Golbot's a different story."

"I know he despises me."

"Golbot doesn't like a lot of things. But he'll come around."

"Let's hope so. They should be here soon."

A shuttle landed on the lawn next to Talisa's ship and Tralin and Golbot announced their arrival at the foyer. Talisa embraced them and they rode the elevator to the top floor where Javensbee stood ready with some trepidation. "Good of you to come, Gentlemen. Make yourselves comfortable."

Dr. Tralin smiled politely. "Thank you, Javensbee. It seems a little odd meeting this way."

Golbot sneered. "Odd ain't the word for it."

"I realize you two don't like me, or trust me. But I assure you, I do not have any ulterior motives."

"Talisa trusts you. That's good enough for us now."

"I have changed. She has seen that change."

Talisa brought them refreshments. "Sit down. We have much to talk about."

Dr. Tralin raised his glass. "To our first meeting together. And I must say, your home is quite impressive."

"Nice, huh?""

Golbot murmured. "I don't see the puffy pink pillows yet."

"You never stop, Golbot." she answered sarcastically. "Who needs entertainment when we have you?"

"It's not everyday we bond with the enemy."

"Hopefully I won't be your enemy forever."

"Sorry, Javensbee. It's hard habit to kick."

Talisa rose from her chair. "I have a good idea. Why don't you and Golbot get to know each other better and Dr. Tralin and I will take a little walk."

"Are you sure, my dear?"

"Yeah, he won't bite."

They left the room and Javensbee smiled pensively at Golbot. "So here we are. Two thousand years of chasing each other and now we're guest and host."

"It does seem impossible."

"But I believe it's a start."

"Tell me, Javensbee, in all our travels, what was our best conquest of you? When did we piss you off the most?"

"You want to know that?"

"Sure. Why not?"

He nodded. "Eight hundred years ago. At Prena 10."

"The zoo?"

"To this day I still don't know how you discovered I was a parasite?"

"We almost didn't. We chased you to the Prena system and you disappeared. At first we thought you were the zookeeper, but then you must have changed forms."

"But how did you know I was a Rubada?"

"We didn't. It's just that the Rubada parasite is very clannish. And there you were, shunned by the rest in the exhibit. We were just about to leave when your girlfriend figured it out."

"Talisa? I should have known. She has shown me that great intuition with her mercenary work."

"We just waited for your move, and that was that."

"I should have fled immediately."

"Your patience betrayed you that time. Besides, we were grateful that the Rubada had such good taste."

"Oh, that's very humorous."

"Speaking about mercenary work; how's that going for you? Must be a little restrictive, mundane."

"Not at all. It has been exhilarating."

As they conversed, Talisa guided Dr. Tralin around the corner of a walkway that overlooked one of the deepest recesses of the canyon. Though dark, they could see the distant mountain peak as a shadow from the thinnest sliver of moonlight. Talisa became quite animated as they stood by the rail. "What's going on, Tralin? I can't keep this up much longer."

"You may not have to."

"What's going on with Ceylar?"

"We were unsuccessful retrieving his past memories. However, Dengy has a bold idea that just may work. Problem is; you're going to have to occupy Javensbee for a short while."

"That may be difficult. We don't have any jobs at the moment."

"You're going to have to think of something. Javensbee must not interfere with this experiment or we could lose everything."

"What is it?"

"Dengy believes that he can recreate the events on the planet Javensbee inside Ceylar's mind as if it were real time."

"How so? He wasn't there."

"Doesn't matter. The particulars are irrelevant since this is going to be a newly created memory. We'll go along with them with virtual processors. Ale will recreate you within the simulation."

"And this is going to work?"

"We don't know. But it's our only hope. Ceylar trusts Dengy and that is our greatest advantage. If we can convince him he is a member of the Mist, then he may be able to complete the bond with the particle link. That should shield him from the shock of waking up from the coma."

"She stared bitterly at the ground. "And this scientist is our only hope? I don't know, Tralin. It better work."

"If Dr. Ceylar believes he's been on this journey and has the power to accelerate the molecular sub-structure; he will react as the Mist."

"And if he doesn't, then I'm stuck with the Songster forever."

"Just get Javensbee out the way for us. We'll do the rest."

"I'll think of something."

When they rejoined Golbot and Javensbee in the house, they were surprised to find them laughing as old friends. Golbot stopped and then pointed his finger at them. "We've been reminiscing about past encounters."

"That's good, because I thought both of you were going crazy."

Javensbee latched his arm around Talisa. "It has been enlightening. And now I'm going to tell you something that none of you were aware of. Something I did to save the galaxy fifteen hundred years ago.

They all gazed at him in silence.

"You recall the incident at Altuistat?"

"Yes, they were developing a cascade weapon of some kind. But it never materialized."

"And so the galaxy had been told. This weapon was not only real, but of a nature far more destructive than anyone had thought possible. I was manipulating the Altuistat people for my own selfish purposes."

Dr. Tralin rubbed his hands together. "We had heard of the weapon, but had no idea you were involved."

"When I examined the weapon, I realized it had the potential to eliminate most of the life in the galaxy. Why would I want to inherit such a dead system?"

"So let me get this straight. You destroyed their weapon?"

"They developed it with their own science. They blindly stumbled on perfection; dubious as it was."

"You still reacted for your own selfish purpose?"

"Yes, Golbot. I once did all things for selfish reasons. But in this case I abandoned my plans and left Altuistat. You soon discovered my whereabouts and exiled me."

"That's what we do best. That is, until recently."

TEN

DENGY WALKED INTO THE STUDY at the college and found Dr. Ceylar comfortably reading a book in his leather chair. He was excited to see Dengy and rose briskly to shake his hand. Dengy's expression was fearful, something Ceylar had never seen on him. "Is there something wrong? You looked worried."

Dengy bit his lip. "To tell you the truth, I am a little worried. Something has happened that is detrimental to all life in our galaxy. It will endanger many families, including my own."

"What could it be?"

"I'm not sure I should burden you with this, considering where you've been."

"Please tell me. You are my friend and if you are troubled, I am too."

"Do you remember me talking about this Songster of Javensbee?"

"I do; in the cave when we first met."

"Dr. Tralin, one of our scientists discovered a very ancient culture; more advanced than anything we know. They're gone now, but they inadvertently created this being that first took the

171

form of weather, and then assumed other abilities. This Javensbee creature became an entity like themselves"

"What happened to it?"

"We think it's here in the galaxy; causing great havoc. It has limitless power."

"What can be done to stop it?"

Dengy held his breath. "We've arranged an expedition to the planet Javensbee. A pilot named Talisa Caru will take us there, along with Golbot of Herenia, a treasure hunter. We think there may be a clue left there on how to defeat this monster. Dr. Tralin is leading the team and we need a geologist. That's where you come in."

Ceylar's mouth dried up. "I don't know, Dengy. There are other well qualified geologists."

"But none I trust, Andropodi."

"It would mean leaving my study. I feel safe here."

"I understand. It's just that we may have to burrow deep into the planet and we need somebody that knows the terrain. Someone that understands the risks so we don't bury ourselves alive."

"Dengy, you saved my life and I am eternally grateful. I'll have to think about it."

"That's all I can ask. I'm really worried about my children; what kind of world they'll grow up in."

"It is a difficult decision for me."

"I know. But you may be our only hope. Think about it and I will return. Now, I must visit my family."

Dengy removed his visor and stared intensely at them. "Now we wait."

* ** * *

Talisa and Javensbee enjoyed a cool evening on the balcony of their estate. She seemed aloof; and just fixed her eyes on the mountaintops. "Talisa, I've been talking to you and you haven't been paying attention to me."

"What's that?"

"Something is disturbing you."

She smiled, kissed him quickly and then backed away. "I've wanted to tell you this, and I guess it's time. It happened when I was a child. I didn't come from a privileged upbringing. My life was always in danger during my early years and it has left an indelible memory."

"Tell me about it."

"I'd rather you see it for yourself. It would mean a lot to me."

"Certainly, my love. If it's that important, we shall go."

"You're not going to like it. The destination is two weeks away."

He exhaled and slumped over. "Naturally, nothing is easy for you. I could just snap my fingers and we'd be there."

"No, I want to take my ship. You still don't understand that I need as normal a life as possible. Once we get there, you'll know why."

He gazed at her suspiciously. "All right. Then we'll do it your way."

They boarded her ship, lifted up over the mountains and out into space. The stars streaked out the window as Javensbee, frustrated at the prospects of another lengthy trip, played around with some of the navigational controls. He knew full well that a future with Talisa meant thousands of plodding journeys just like this. He loved Talisa, but always considered himself a leader, not a follower.

Wary of a negative response, Dengy prepared himself for Ceylar's decision. "I'm going in." He opened the door to the study and Dr. Ceylar sulked in his chair with the dourest of expressions. Every dreadful emotion shot through Dengy's muscles as he waited for an answer.

"I want to stay here in the safe confines of my study, but I realize that no place will be safe with this creature. I owe you my life, Dengy. I've decided to agree to join your expedition."

He ran over to Ceylar and embraced him. "Thank you, Andropdi. And my family thanks you."

"When do we leave?"

"Wait here. I'm going to gather the others. We must leave soon."

"I'll be here."

Dengy ripped off the visor exuberantly. "He agreed!"

Dr. Tralin almost collapsed in relief. "We may yet succeed."

Golbot's cheeks swelled with air. "I knew the old guy would do it. Now I have to get use to calling him Andropdi."

Dizzy and restless, Dengy stood in the middle of the lab. "Let's get the equipment into Golbot's ship. Ale, you secure Dr. Ceylar for the ride. Golbot, have you found a suitable planet to substitute for Javensbee?"

"It took a little investigating to find the right balance of oxygen and gravity, but the Prilo Foisa system is perfect."

"Good. The equipment should be up and running when we leave Benari."

Dr. Tralin smiled warmly at Ale. "That husband of yours is something else.'

She stared lovingly at Dengy. "He has his moments."

Javensbee was already bored on the ride through the darkness. He respected Talisa, but felt restricted and controlled. He knew that compromise in a relationship was important, but that compromise went both ways. Hour after hour his patience was tested beyond what he could endure.

Dengy supervised the loading of scientific equipment as Dr. Ceylar was lifted onto Golbot's ship. In a few short hours they calibrated all the virtual machinery necessary for group interaction. Ale had preprogrammed an impersonation of the likeness of Talisa Caru and Dengy had linked all the processors to the main power source. Their objective was to convince Ceylar they were all on this journey together.

Golbot set the course to Prilo Foisa, placed the controls on auto-navigation and took his seat at the virtual processor. Dengy gave them final instructions. "Now remember at all times it is two thousands year ago. Things were a lot different. This was before beaming down to planets and traveling at quantified warp. Even the geological equipment reflects the period. We must always remain in character; and whatever you do, always refer to him as Andropodi."

"We can manage that."

"I think we're ready."

Golbot stopped them. "I just thought of something. Since Ceylar has been physically repaired, what if he wakes up from his coma?"

"That's a remote possibility. He doesn't know he's in coma and it's highly unlikely that his sub-conscious protective barriers even would allow it."

They all sat at their processor outlets and placed the visors over their heads. Dengy activated the system and walked into the study alone. "Dengy, I'm ready."

"My friends are outside. I'll invite them in."

Dr. Ceylar anticipated the group's arrival and Dengy led the three of them into the room. "Andropodi, this is Dr. Tralin, Golbot and our pilot, Talisa Caru." They all embraced Ceylar enthusiastically.

"It's an honor to meet you all."

"My spaceship is parked on your lawn outside. I hope that's okay. We're really going to need a geologist where we're going."

"Miss Caru, I'd do anything for my friend, Dengy."

For the first time Dr. Ceylar left his study, strolled out onto the lawn and entered a facsimile of the vessel that Talisa had piloted on that first expedition. Ale went up to the cockpit and pretended to set course for Javensbee. The ship rose off the campus grounds, shot upwards between two stately towers and accelerated into space at warp speeds.

The real Talisa Caru and Javensbee sped towards a planet that would provide the setting for her ruse. After two days travel time, Javensbee was beginning to show agitation and impatience. She could sense his frustration, but had little choice but to engage him in friendly conversation. After awhile, he slammed his fist on the control panel.

"What's wrong?"

"What's wrong is that I've been doing all the compromising and you have not reciprocated."

"I didn't realize you felt this way."

"I don't mind going to this forsaken planet of yours, but I see no reason prolonging the journey."

"What do you propose?"

He snapped his fingers and the ship covered the vast lacuna of space in seconds and arrived at her planet. "This is what I mean by compromise. Now you may show me your childhood secrets."

She pursed her lips. "You're right. Now if you don't mind, we'll do it my way from now on."

"I can hardly wait."

"We're going to establish orbit and beam down. Get ready for a lot of walking."

"Typical. I've scanned this sphere and find it lacking in population centers."

"There are scattered villages. Some tribal communities. But you're right. This place hasn't changed much since my childhood."

The virtual spacecraft dropped to sub-light speed and aimed towards a small gray and reddish brown planet orbiting a yellow star. "Our first look at Javnsbee", Tralin announced excitedly. "What do you think, Andropodi?"

"It appears lifeless."

"You're right. Nobody lives there now. But we believe this was once the home of a very advanced civilization."

"Where are we setting down?"

Golbot pointed. "The southern hemisphere. That's where

the buried city is supposed to be. Your job is to find the best way in."

"And how do I do that?"

"Scan for open caverns. My first scan of this place showed the planet's riddled with them. When Tralin found out about these tales, he hired me."

"Plot a search pattern and I'll begin my scans."

Ale maneuvered the ship over a rocky, hilly region of the southern hemisphere that Dr. Ceylar analyzed with the familiar equipment of his day. He looked for anomalous readings, but didn't find anything unusual. Eventually a heat sensor detected a vast open area one mile below the surface.

"It's a cave system, all right. A labyrinth of tunnels. I'd say many of them indicate they are not natural formations."

"That could be our ruins."

"Fits the category. But definitely no life signs."

Dr. Tralin turned away and scrubbed his jaw. "Then we're here. This is where we're going to dig. Any surface access?"

"Doesn't appear to be. There seems to be some kind of shaft close to the surface. We can gain access there. It's not a steep decline once we're inside. The composition is sandstone, iron, and felsite; typical for this class of planet."

"Let's set down."

The real Talisa beamed down with Javensbee to the windy planet where dust particles pelted their faces immediately. The clouds were high and thin and the atmosphere was dusty gray. Javensbee flinched. "So this is what you wanted to show me?"

"Not exactly. We have about a twenty mile walk."

"And you're sure you don't want me to shorten the trip?"

"No, you're missing the point. It's the journey that's going to help you understand what I went through."

"Always a difficult way for my Talisa."

"Let's go; between those hills."

Ale landed the ship on the virtual planet's surface. "Here we are at Javensbee. The garden spot of the universe."

Golbot laughed. "Let's get the rig out."

Dengy assisted Dr. Ceylar with parts of the laser boring equipment which they assembled a short distance away from a low pebbly bluff. The drill had a one foot circumference on the end of a bulky machine which was aimed at the middle section of the bluff. "The first blast will probably clear the loose stuff. Once that's accomplished, we can think about boring a more precise hole."

"You're in charge."

The drill blasted a concave hole and the pebbles and sandstone immediately collapsed and buried it. The second more powerful blast cleared the remainder of the debris and began to penetrate into more stable rock. The second hole eventually collapsed, but the third hole drilled at a twenty-five degree angle penetrated solid granite and bedrock; and left a wide entry into the bluff.

"Now we can move inside and break through the shaft wall. That should take us right into the cave."

Javenbsee was becoming more impatient with every step. With the exception of scattered brush and one or two flying reptiles, there wasn't much else around. They had hiked five miles and he stopped her. "This is absurd, Talisa. Where are we going?"

"A village. A small village. When you meet these people, you'll understand my bleak origins."

"And what could that possibly tell me?"

"Javensbee, have I ever let you down before?"

"You really want me to answer that?"

Dengy was the first to climb down the shaft that was steep in sections. The shaft narrowed considerably until crawling was the only way through. "Can we drill inside here?"

"I wouldn't recommend it. It's pretty unstable in places. Igneous, metamorphic, mud rock, recrystallization. A recipe for disaster."

"Then on our stomachs we go."

Using flashlights, they slithered and squirmed through the

opening. "I'm in", shouted Dengy. "It's about ten feet tall and getting bigger."

One by one they scraped their knees and reached the tunnel which expanded into an actual cavern. Ale aimed a pistol up at the ceiling. "This product was just invented. It lights up dark surfaces." She glanced over at Tralin.

"Yes, it's an excellent invention. It's called…corbolite."

Andropodi hunched his shoulders. "Never heard of it."

One shot from Ale's pistol illuminated the cave ceiling and revealed ruins of a lost civilization. There were partial sections of stone and metallic buildings with junky debris pilled up against the surfaces. At the far end of the cave was another tunnel entrance in the side of the wall. Unable to find the creature they hunted, they stepped over piles of debris and made their way to the other side of the cave. At first the tunnel was cramped, but then it widened considerably and opened up into a huge cave that housed the ruins of a massive city.

They shot the corbolite at the ceiling. "Look at this place!"

Andropodi studied the readings. "Over one hundred thousand years old."

"No signs of life."

They climbed among piles of rubble where only a few wall structures even reached two stories in height. Golbot stopped them. "Wait a minute. I'm getting an energy reading."

"Where?"

"Over there. About five hundred feet."

They rummaged through the gutted rooms of a few buildings until they came upon a courtyard where a strange, unimpressive metallic pole protruded from the dirt. On top of the pole was a cheaply painted red and white ten sided star configuration with a single yellow eye in the center. Golbot took another reading. "Believe it or not, this is the energy source."

"That stupid looking thing?"

"I'm telling you, this is the source."

Javensbee followed Talisa through the canyon, still wondering

179

why this was all necessary. He suddenly grabbed her arm when he heard a rustling up in the rocky terrain above. "Are you expecting friends? We seem to have company."

She gazed upward. "No friends of mine."

"Who are they?"

"Got no idea." She spotted several of them on the top of the ridge. "But it's a safe bet they're bandits."

"Bandits? Is this what you encountered as a child?"

"Yes. They were brutal. Maybe they'll ignore us."

He pointed up the trail. "I doubt that very much."

Ahead were eight surly men blocking their path; the largest of them standing in front with arms folded. Never shy, Talisa headed right for them. "It appears to be our welcoming committee."

"Not exactly your friendly types."

The seven foot tall, muscular, tattooed leader snarled ferociously with saliva dripping down his chin. The others wore painted garments and had gaudy jewelry piercing their bodies. The leader stood erect with arms folded as the rest aimed weapons at them. "What do we have here", he spoke in a low, hoarse voice. "Lost vacationers? Missionaries?"

Javensbee stepped ahead of Talisa. "We don't want any trouble."

The leader turned around and laughed. "He doesn't want any trouble."

Talisa nudged in front of Javensbee. "Really, you don't want to anger my friend."

He pointed. "That puny little crap?"

"He may look pathetic, but he can handle himself quite well."

"You're a pretty little thing. You'll do well as my sex slave. After I rip every piece of flesh off your friend, I'm going to have a lot of fun with you."

Javensbee became slightly annoyed. "That's it." He stepped back in front of her. "We told you we didn't want any trouble. We don't have anything of wealth on us, so just let us pass."

"We've been watching you for an hour. You are alone; no vessel, no villagers. I'd say you're in big trouble."

Javensbee pulled Talisa aside. "This has gone far enough. Let me dispense with these idiots and we'll be on our way."

"All right. But we're going to do it my way."

"Oh no, not again. What now?"

"A fair fight."

He stood aback, insulted. "What do you mean, fair fight?"

"Strength matching strength. This barbarian has been indignant with me and now it's time to fight for your woman's honor."

"Me? You can take every one of them."

She moseyed over to the side of the path, sat down on a rock and crossed her legs. "All right, boys. He's all yours."

Exasperated, Javensbee sauntered up to the leader and grinned. "It appears I must fight you. So I give you a final warning."

He turned to his gang. "The pipsqueak's going to fight me."

They chuckled; the leader smiled and punched Javensbee in the mouth, sending him backwards onto his buttocks. They all laughed as the leader pointed over at Talisa. "You'd better take those clothes off now bitch. Or I'll have to make it more unpleasant for you later."

"Now you've really made him mad."

Javenbsee dusted himself off and gazed at Talisa. "I really have to make this fair? I hate to touch this...thing."

"I'll make it quick and painless for your puny ass."

Javensbee stood up defiant and raised his fists in a fighting stance. The leader burst out laughing and threw a punch, which Javensbee deflected. He threw another punch which was also deflected and finally three more before Javensbee's fist struck squarely in the center of the leader's mouth. Surprised, the leader wiped the blood off his lip, became enraged and charged at him. Javensbee leaped aside quickly and whacked him in the ribs, tripped him and sent him crashing to the ground.

Talisa cheered from the side. "You guys had enough?"

The leader snarled at her, propped himself up off the ground and charged one more time. Javensbee kicked him twice in the stomach, grabbed his neck and twisted it violently. The cracking sound horrified the rest of the gang as their leader fell lifeless to the ground. In a sudden charge they too confronted Javensbee with clubs and knives. He easily deflected all the flailing weaponry and smashed his fist into their faces and broke their bones.

Javensbee glanced over at Talisa, who was still seated comfortably on the rock. "You're not joining in?" he asked.

"No lover, you're doing just fine."

Three of them stood amidst the fallen; one ran off, the other two, confused and breathing heavily, shouted like wounded animals and charged with less enthusiasm. He grabbed one of their arms and ripped it out the socket and slammed his fist several times into his face until it was unrecognizable. The other one fled.

Talisa clapped her hands. "We did warn them."

"Disgusting that I had to interact with them in this lowly manner."

"I have to give you credit. You used skill against skill. Turns out you're pretty good at this kind of combat."

"That insult was unnecessary. It was a display of brutality."

"Brutality? And the massacre at Katus was clinical?"

He raised a brow. "Bring that up. So now that I saved my woman, how does that make you feel?"

"Kind of good."

"Don't get use to it."

"That should be the last of the bandits for a while."

"Talisa, let me ask you something. I haven't seen any villages or villagers this whole time. What are we doing out here?"

"You said you trusted me. I have something to show you and it's not far from here."

"Let's get on with it."

Dengy and the expedition team encircled the pole and

it emitted a whistling sound. The painted eye on top of the pole began to pulsate with a yellow glow and the ground shook mildly as they exchanged quick glances. The whistling ended and blinding white beams propelled out in every direction. A mellow voice spoke to them. "You are the first to come to this planet; a planet we have designated as Javensbee." Ale stared at Dengy as if to relay her sense of corniness. "Long ago we have lived in the galaxy, moving from place to place, discovering species that one day would populate many worlds. We traveled by thought and energy. Our scientists had developed methods to control time and space, but we were careless and created a being that possessed our abilities, yet without our cultural restraints. At first it used the weather on this planet to assimilate a life from, but it gained knowledge quickly. We have waited for individuals to countermand those abilities. Javensbee will not be able to overpower, or overcome you because you will be four times his strength. It is difficult for you to understand, but the properties we endow you with will give you immortality. You can not destroy this evil beast, but you can repel him. Your limited minds, you're inability to travel inter-dimensionally in time will protect you from his inquisition. You shall be called the Mist, for you will be like a mist to him."

The whistling sound started again and a purplish glow engulfed all of them for a few seconds, and then it vanished. The yellow glow in the eye on top of the pole faded and the city once again was completely silent.

"What just happened?"

"I don't know, Andropodi. I don't feel any different."

An unexpected wind formed west of the cavern and swirled in a tornado next to the pole. It took humanoid shape and then stopped twisting to form the recognizable Javensbee. He just stood there, grinning.

"I take it you are Javensbee?"

"I am. And you pitiful creatures have no means to stop me." He snapped his fingers and Ale lifted off the ground and was flown right out of the cave in a powerful wind that stirred up rock and dust. Panicked, Dr. Tralin pointed over to the cave exit. They scurried out the main cave, into the smaller second cave and finally into the shaft that led to the surface. When they arrived, Ale was suspended in mid-air.

"Let her go!"

Javensbee dropped her to the ground. "You have no persuasion over me. Now it is my turn to rule the galaxy." With the wave of his arm he rendered all of them unconscious. Dengy turned off the processor. "The moment of truth, my friends. It's time we remove Dr. Ceylar and put him on the real planet."

They floated him out of the ship and brought him to the shaft entrance which had been duplicated for real on the planet's surface. They laid him on the ground as he would have fallen and Ale programmed a holographic curtain to hide Golbot's actual ship. Dengy removed a small device to bring Dr. Ceylar out of the coma. "If there was anything more we could have done, I don't know what it could have been."

"Do you think we can revive him?"

"Everything medically has been repaired. Nothing left but to activate this device. Dr. Ceylar will think that he's just come out of Javensbee's stun."

Dengy placed the device on Ceylar's forehead and Tralin touched his body. Dengy instructed them to lie on the ground in the position they had fallen. He activated the device, put it away in his pocket and also stretched out on the ground. They watched for the first sign of Dr. Ceylar's eyebrows fluttering and then he slowly opened his eyes. They too opened their eyes and stood up along side him.

Golbot glanced around anxiously. "Where's Talisa?"

"He must have taken her."

Ceylar walked towards the holographic ship facade. "We must rescue her."

Dengy shouted. "No!"

"What do you mean?"

"We're the Mist. We have to save her that way."

Tralin clutched onto Dengy's wrist. "You don't think that was all true?"

"There's only one way to find out." Dengy opened his palm and tried to conjure up the purplish glow. "Nothing happened."

Golbot opened his palm and the light appeared. Dr. Tralin did the same and then they all fixed their eyes on Dr. Ceylar.

The real Talisa Caru led Javensbee through the canyon pass, spying the cliffs for any more bandits. She kept quiet, but could sense his impatience.

He stopped. "Talisa, we've gone far enough."

"What do you mean?"

"There is no village, no childhood drama."

"Why do you say that?"

"This had been a charade. A distraction. The question is, why?"

"It's just around the bend."

She could see anger rising in him. "Tell me what is happening."

She signed and responded with a surrendering frown. "You're right. This has nothing to do with my childhood."

"Then why are we here?"

"I guess it doesn't matter any more. Sooner or later you're going to find out. We have been unsuccessful."

"So this was deception? To bring back Ceylar, perhaps?"

She was about to confess when she peered over his shoulder and began to smile. He blinked, turned around and was startled to find the other three members of the Mist standing behind him.

"How can this be?"

Dr. Tralin nodded confidently. "This time you were the victim."

"So it appears." He turned back to Talisa in sorrow. "I didn't expect this from you. I trusted you. I loved you."

"Javensbee, you may not believe this, but I had fallen for you, too. It had been so long since I had those feelings."

"Then perhaps we can still be together?"

"You know that's not going to happen."

He spoke in a pleading tone. "I really have changed. You've seen it."

"We operate in two different worlds. In my world, there's good and evil; no gray area. It's not a little good, or a lot of good; or for that matter, a little evil, and a lot of evil. You Javensbee, for lack of a complex explanation, are evil."

"But you have witnessed my transformation."

"Have I? It's only a matter of time before you tire of me and my way of life. Soon you'll lose your patience with all of us inferior creatures. And I think that time has already come."

"I've given you no reason to believe that."

"No reason, yet. But be honest with me. You already hate this way of life. Perhaps it's only a matter of days before you would have discarded me."

His conciliatory behavior turned to smugness. "Yes, you're right. I am not meant to be a servant. And that is what I've become. And yet of all your talk of good, it was evil to deceive me."

"Songster, you are the exception to any rule when it comes to evil. For you have the power to unilaterally decide everyone's fate."

"I have learned a valuable lesson that I will never repeat. Trusting anyone else is a tragic mistake. That will never happen again."

"Fortunately, you know where you're going now."

Javensbee lifted his index finger with authority. "Know this you who call yourselves the saviors of the galaxy. I will never be defeated. And what little caring I had for you Talisa is over. It has been replaced by hatred, something I am very familiar with. It is obvious that I will never have dominance in my home galaxy as long as the Mist is here. It's now time to search out other galaxies. Who knows, there may be a civilization even more powerful than all of us that can destroy the Mist once and for all. The next time I return I will not come alone."

Golbot belched. "Are you through?"

Javensbee smiled with a sinister glare.

The four of them simultaneously produced a purplish glow and Javensbee began to morph from a humanoid into the brightly illuminated outline of a face. His eyes flushed blood red and his scowl resembled a tortured soul. He hung in the air as a white mass until the brilliance overcame his facial features. He opened what appeared to be his mouth, let out a horrible shrieking scream and jettisoned away into space with a comet's tail.

As calmly as could be, Dr. Ceylar whispered under his breath. "He's gone."

Talisa chuckled in relief. "I guess I'm stuck with all of you again."

Golbot laughed. "Not too late to chase down lover boy."

"Funny. I can always rely on you for comic relief." She walked towards Dr. Ceylar until Tralin tugged on her shirt.

"Andropodi is just fine."

She understood. "Yes. Well, it's good to have peace again. And thank you all for rescuing me."

"I'd say it's Javensbee that needs rescuing."

Dr. Tralin put his arm around Ceylar's shoulder. "My friend, we have much to discuss. It will take some time. But the four of us will always be the Mist. That is something that can not be taken away from us."

"I'll beam us up to my ship." She gazed back with mixed feelings at the spot where Javensbee had departed.

* ** * *

Dengy shuffled briskly down the translucent corridors of the Benarian scientific institution. Passing by rows of black doors and whipping around a couple of corners, he entered into Dr.

Tralin's former office. Tralin had been waiting for him as he packed what was left of his personal items. "Dengy, good to see you. Come in."

"I'm a little disappointed that you're retiring for real this time."

He shook his head in amazement. "You still don't understand the magnitude of what you've done."

"What do you mean?"

"You saved the galaxy. You're a hero. And not just some ordinary hero. No one else in history has done what you have."

"It was the Mist."

"The Mist? We would have failed. We were powerless. You and your beautiful wife were the ones that saved us all. You are a hero like none other; and regrettably a hero that will never be recorded in history. Your triumph, the deeds you accomplished; only the few will know. I'm sorry, Dengy. But it has to be that way."

"I understand."

"At one time the Mist considered going public. But we decided that wouldn't be right. The accolades that would accompany fame; adulation, unlimited powers, are the very things our adversary yearns for. So we just operate in the shadows, quietly protecting others."

"I'm just grateful that my family is safe."

"There is some good news, Dengy. Your scientific breakthroughs will now give you much deserved recognition. You'll have a long career here at the institution. They'll all have confidence in you now."

"I'll probably be spending my remaining years devising safeguards against memory manipulation. By the way, how is Dr. Ceylar doing?"

"He's coming along fine. He wanted me to tell you he appreciated everything you did for him."

"How much does he know?"

"We told him everything. He knows everything. It is difficult, but He is taking it well. He understands why we needed to create a new memory. And he is comfortable now as one of the Mist."

"What will happen to you? Where will you go?"

He turned away and faced the wall. "I will retire, travel the galaxy, and then in a few years will meet with some kind of accident. The memory of the Dr. Tralin will eventually subside."

"And then what?"

"I will find a new identity, like all of us. Maybe this time an ordinary being with no particular accomplishments. That's the way it is with us. We become noticed and then we fade to obscurity. It's the best way."

"I'm going to miss you."

"I'll miss you, too. Is there anything else? You look unsettled."

"I can't help but to think this whole thing is too coincidental."

"How so?"

"Here you are; eternal beings. And then there's the Songster. And then I come along, your employee, the only one that can save the Mist and the galaxy. I just happen to be at the right place at the right time."

He nodded empathetically. "I think I understand what you're asking. Is there a greater power? Perhaps, even God?"

"I do believe there is a God."

"Dengy, you might be surprised that I'm a believer, too. I've lived over two thousand years and I've seen amazing coincidences. But this one is beyond my fathoming. But I know two things for sure. Everything does not come from nothing. And science has never proven what is before the beginning."

* **

Dengy chased his youngest son through the foliage of the wooded planet he had so often visited. The boy laughed, giggled, hid among the trees, dashed out from behind boulders and ran along a churning stream. Dengy finally caught up to him among a patch of wildflowers and swooped him up in the air, swinging him from side to side. "Come on, it's getting dark. Mom will have dinner ready soon."

"Dad, do we have to?"

He set him down. "You know your mom."

"All right..."

Ale and her oldest daughter were at the campsite cooking over an outdoor stove. Her daughter brought marinated meat from the shelter's freezer and handed it to her mom. "Oh, these look delicious."

"Can I go find dad?"

"No, they'll be back any minute."

She whined softly. "Oh, mom."

Dengy and their boy emerged from the forest and the he ran towards Ale. The sun was just setting and the birds sang their last lullaby in the trees.

"Did you have fun?"

"Yeah. We played soldiers."

Dengy's daughter held onto his hand. "Hi, baby. You going fishing with us tomorrow?"

"Yeah."

"That means we can't stay up late."

Mother banged on a plate. "Let's eat. I know everybody's hungry."

They ran up to the table and Dengy slipped his arm around his wife. "This is so perfect. You don't know how long I dreamed of these moments."

"Me too."

"I remember my parents taking me here. And now I have my own kids."

"You're really happy now."

"What's not be happy about."

"Get your plate."

Dengy joined his children with plate in hand and Ale served them. They sat together at the table and relished every bite. Ale reached over to Dengy with a napkin and wiped the side of his mouth. The children glommed down the food and sipped their drinks.

"Mom, when we get back home can I come back here with my friends?"

"We're here now, and you want to go right back?"

"Well, yeah."

"If your father says it's all right."

"Son, we'll talk about it when we get home."

They finished eating and the last glimmer of light filtered through the treetops. Ale and her daughter cleaned up the site while Dengy and his son gathered firewood. After sorting through the thickest logs, he arranged them over the fire pit and put the smaller twigs on top. Soon the flames kept them warm as they listened to the crying animals in the distance. They told stories and played word games until Ale reminded her children it was bedtime. They at first resisted, but Dengy eventually tucked them away securely in the shelter.

"Don't stay up late. We have early fishing."

He returned to the fire pit and sat next to Ale. "No regrets, Dengy?"

"We have a new lab, new friends, what's to regret?"

"I just thought you might miss the action."

"Don't be silly. This is what's real."

"I love you. Thanks for being such a good husband and father."

"I love you too, Ale."

"Well, I think we all should go to bed. I got a few things to put away."

"I'll join you soon."

Dengy leaned back in his chair, closed his eyes and was hypnotized by the crackling flames. An ember popped out, startling him for a second; but he was again lulled into tranquility.

He sniffed the clean air, gazed upward into the night and followed a few shooting stars that burned out with little fanfare. One meteor even appeared particularly bright with a longer tail before it vanished forever.